Confidentially YOURS

Vanessa's Fashion Face-Off

2

ALSO BY JO WHITTEMORE

Confidentially Yours #1: Brooke's Not-So-Perfect Plan

JO WHITTEMORE

Confidentially

YOURS

Vanessa's Fashion Face-Off

2

HARPER

An Imprint of HarperCollinsPublishers

Library of Congress Control Number:
2015938986
ISBN 978-0-06-235895-0

Typography by Kate J. Engbring
15 16 17 18 19   OPM   10 9 8 7 6 5 4 3 2 1
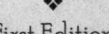
First Edition

For Uncle Rick,
who showed me Chicago

Contents

Confidentially YOURS

Vanessa's Fashion Face-Off

2

CHAPTER 1

Fashion Passion

This was the night I'd been waiting for.

With one hand I pulled back a glossy blue curtain and squinted against the stage lights for a glimpse at the audience—A-list celebs chatted on folding chairs, Badgley Mischka and Birkin bags tucked under their seats. Some of them saw me and whispered excitedly, waving and snapping photos with their phones.

I grinned and humored them with a pose before retreating backstage. No time to flaunt; I had models to prep for the runway.

The models gathered for inspection, each

wearing a piece from my new fall line. I paused in front of one and adjusted her shoulder strap for a better silhouette.

Glancing at my watch, I ushered the models to follow the choreographer and readied myself at the side of the stage.

The master of ceremonies winked at me, raised his microphone, and said, "Little girl, can you ask your brother to stop licking the window?"

"Huh?"

I blinked, and the runway disappeared, replaced by a ball gown–wearing mannequin in a store window display. And I wasn't backstage in Paris. I was on the sidewalk in Chicago, glancing up at a man in a sharp black suit accessorized with ... a security badge.

"I said, can you ask your brother to stop licking the window?" he repeated. "I'm assuming he is your brother."

He pointed to a young boy standing inside the display, tongue pressed to the glass like a dog slobbering on a porch screen.

My first impulse was to say, "No, sir, I do *not* know that kid waving at us!" and run through traffic to escape.

But since my brother, Terrell, and I look so much alike—same dimples, same wild Afros, same gold-flecked eyes—there was nothing I could do but sigh.

"Yes, sir. I'll get him."

I turned to go inside and then stopped in front of the revolving entry door.

"Well?" pressed the security guard.

"Uh . . . I'm not . . ."

I wasn't sure how to finish. He wouldn't believe me if I told him revolving doors were my enemies. Actually, doors in general were my enemies. And corners of furniture. And gravity.

I'm kind of clumsy.

"Never mind," I said. "Wish me luck."

Sure enough, as the door went around, I misjudged the opening and barely squeezed through in time, losing a shoe in the process.

"Crud." I hopped on one foot, waiting for an opening and then leaping into the space between two panels just as the security guard went around the other side, holding my shoe. "Double crud!"

I was so glad nobody from Abraham Lincoln Middle School could see this, especially my teammates at "Lincoln's Letters," our school newspaper's advice column. Besides working together, those three were also my best friends, and I knew exactly how they'd react.

Brooke Jacobs, our tomboy with fiery-red hair, would've injected some sort of sports commentary.

Heather Schwartz—our adorable, gaptoothed songbird—would've said, "Oh, sweetie!"

and taken off one of her shoes so I wouldn't feel so bad.

And Tim Antonides—our tall, dark-haired comedian—would've joked, "The revolving door god is pleased with your offering."

Since they weren't around, I quietly accepted my shoe from the security guard, slipped it on, and went inside. Terrell giggled when he saw me and sprinted behind a clothes rack.

"Terrell!" I whispered as loud as I dared. "Get back here or I won't play Battle the Mermaid with you anymore!"

It was a game my brother came up with that's basically hide-and-seek with his special treasures. I, the mermaid, steal them, and he has to get them back. Since I'm allowed to dress up, I don't complain about playing.

My brother scampered over, and I scooted him toward the door, holding the belt loop at the back of his jeans.

"Why were you licking the window?" I asked.

"I wasn't licking the window!" He shot me an offended look. "I was making a tongue print."

I busted out laughing. I couldn't help it.

If someone asked my friends to describe me, they'd probably say I was overly cheerful and positive, especially given the number of ridiculous things that happen to me on a daily basis. I don't think that's a bad thing. It's better than being the girl who cries if she spills something on her favorite top.

Don't get me wrong; fashion disasters aren't to be taken lightly, but you can either sulk or solve the problem. And I always choose to set things right.

I nodded to the security guard, who stood in front of the revolving door and gestured to one side.

A regular door next to the revolving one. Imagine.

I smiled at him. "Now we're talking!"

My brother, who had no idea what was going on, ignored both of us and pushed through the door to step outside.

Our car was already there, and Mom was leaning across to shout out the passenger window.

"Come on, you two! I'm blocking traffic!"

Terrell and I ran over, me hopping into the front seat and him into the back.

"I'm sorry that took so long," said Mom. "Getting out of the garage was a nightmare."

"It's Michigan Ave.," I told her. "If there's no traffic, it's the apocalypse."

Michigan Avenue, aka the Magnificent Mile, was famous for its stores, restaurants, and hotels. Normally, Mom wouldn't leave Berryville, the nearby suburb where we live, to venture out among the hundreds of tourists and shoppers, but she'd wanted to visit my grandma at her retirement home in the city. And while we were there,

Grandma had given me something extra special for my Halloween costume.

For someone who loves fashion as much as I do, Halloween is like Christmas and my birthday rolled into one. A chance to dress up and get rewarded for it with candy. But this year the candy wasn't even the big draw. This year it was the Schwartzes' Halloween party. For the first time, Heather, Brooke, Tim, and I would be old enough to attend, and if the stories Heather's older brothers told were true, the party would be epic.

I'd been working on my costume since mid-summer, and with a week to go, it was almost done. I'd just needed one last piece, which I'd picked up today at Grandma's: a Victorian cameo brooch with the carving of a young woman's face in it. Grandma made me swear up and down that I wouldn't lose it and that I'd go to church with her because she loves going and wearing fancy hats. (I guess my fashion bug had to come from somewhere.)

By the time we got home, it was dark, and Terrell was passed out cold in the backseat. Mom hoisted him over one shoulder.

"Could you bring in the bags, please?" She popped the trunk and moved some For Sale signs that had fallen on them.

Mom's a Realtor, which I love because she gets to "dress" homes to show off to potential buyers *and* she bakes cookies that Terrell and I get to sample before open houses. People weren't sure she could make it on her own after my dad passed away, and that was before Terrell was even born. But my mom showed the world how strong a woman can be, and she's one of the main reasons I want to make a name for myself. Like mother, like daughter!

Mom carried Terrell inside, and I grabbed the bags, clutching hers in one hand and my four in the other, wishing I'd put on my gloves. It was only October, but the nights were already getting chilly. Still, I loved how it added to the spookiness of the season.

I closed the trunk and turned around.

A pale face popped up in front of mine.

"Hey!" it said.

"Augh! Child ghost!" I flailed my arms, shopping bags whipping back and forth. One of the bags struck the ghost squarely in the shoulder.

"Ow!"

Whoops. Solid body? Not a ghost.

"Sorry!" I said, lowering the bags.

"Oh gosh, no, *I'm* sorry!" The mystery girl rubbed her arm. "In my head, this was supposed to be friendly, not frightening."

"Are you okay?" I asked.

She rotated her shoulder. "I think so. Luckily, I only use this arm for holding purses."

I wasn't sure if she was joking, so I glanced

up and down the street. "Where did you come from?"

"Los Angeles," she said.

I laughed. "No, I meant just now."

"Oh!" She laughed too. "My folks and I just moved in across the street."

She pointed to a blue two-story with an SUV in the driveway.

"You came from California with all your stuff in that?" I asked.

She made a face. And then an entire road trip's worth of conversation came out.

"Actually, a moving van was with us, but it broke down, steaming, smoking . . . the works!" She threw her hands in the air for emphasis. "So it's still a day behind. We packed some extra clothes in the car because you never know what state calls for what outfit; like, for California, you need a sweater, but in Arizona you don't, but in Colorado you do! So we didn't have any room for dishware, and my parents are supereco and don't believe in plastic forks, so they wanted me to ask if you had three regular ones we could borrow."

I blinked as my brain caught up with her words. "Three . . . forks?"

She nodded. "Nonplastic, please."

"Uh . . . sure! Follow me," I said, adjusting my bags. "I'm Vanessa, by the way."

"Katie," she said. "Here, let me help." She eyed the label on one of the bags she grabbed. "You went shopping at Fitzhugh's? I love that store!"

"Me too!" I said. "They have the best leggings."

"The best," she agreed. Then she gasped and held up another bag. "And you went to Barneys? You must be swimming in the green. Is your pool filled with twenties?"

I laughed again. "No, I buy stuff on sale and then rework it into something better. Fashion is kind of my passion."

Katie squealed and threw her arms around me. "Mine too!" She immediately stepped back. "Sorry! That was weird since we haven't even exchanged forks. But I'm so happy to meet some-one my age—at least, I'm assuming you're my age?"

"I'm twelve," I said.

"Me too!" She bounced up and down. "And I'm also assuming you probably hate polyester?"

"It's the worst!" I said, and we both laughed.

The front door opened and Mom poked her head out. "Vanessa?" She spotted Katie and opened the door wider. "Well, hello there!"

"Mom, this is Katie," I said, nudging my new friend closer to the door. "She and her folks moved in across the street, but their stuff hasn't got here yet. Can they borrow some forks?"

"I think we can do a little better than that," said Mom with a wink. "Come inside, girls."

Katie and I followed Mom into the kitchen.

Now that there was more light, I could see that Katie was definitely a girl after my own heart. She was wearing black satiny harem pants with a white crop top. I personally would've added a blue scarf to bring out the color of her eyes, but for someone who'd just traveled halfway across the country, she looked good.

Mom grabbed a basket from the pantry and set it on the counter. "Give me a second to put together a little something for your parents," she said to Katie.

Katie nodded. "Thank you, Ms. . . ."

"Jackson," I supplied. "Can you hand me those bags?" I nodded to the ones Katie was holding. "Unless you want to follow me to my room."

Katie nodded again, still wide-eyed. "I'd love to see your reworked clothes."

I stared at her, awestruck. "Really?"

This was a designer's dream: a request to

see their work. Mind you, the requestor was a twelve-year-old girl who wasn't going to carry my label and make me rich, but I'd take what I could get.

"Can I show Katie my stuff?" I asked Mom.

She smiled. "I'll holler for you when I'm done here."

Katie followed me down the hall, and when I flipped on the light to my room, she gasped and ran up to one of my walls. "I love this!"

The whole wall was nothing but cork, so it looked like a giant bulletin board. I'd pinned magazine pages and sketches I'd drawn on one half, and tacked up photos of family and friends on the other.

"The real wall is still behind it," I said. "This is just paneling."

"And who are these girls?" She pointed to one of many photos of Brooke, Heather, and me.

"Those are my best friends from school," I said. "We write an advice column for our school paper, the *Lincoln Log*. Brooke writes about sports and fitness"—I pointed to her—"and Heather writes about relationships and friendships." I pointed her out in a different picture, along with Tim. "And Tim writes the guy's perspective."

"And you write about fashion?" asked Katie. "Brilliant idea to showcase your talent!"

"Well, Brooke gets the credit," I said. "The newspaper needed some space filled, and she suggested it. She's always excited to try new things."

I left out the part where Brooke's overeagerness had overwhelmed her in the first month of school and that we were lucky to even still have her on the paper.

"But I bet you're the best columnist," said

Katie. "Or at least . . . the best dressed!"

"But of course!" I presented one of my tops with a flourish.

Katie oohed and aahed appropriately, inspecting the stitching. "This is so professional! You have got to be the coolest person I've ever met, Vanessa."

I beamed. "Thanks. I put a lot of blood, sweat, and tears into each piece."

That wasn't just a figure of speech, either. Learning to use a needle was a painful process.

Katie toyed with the sleeve of one of the tops and asked, almost bashfully, "Want to see some of my work?"

I wrinkled my forehead. "I thought your moving van—"

"No, on my website. Do you have a computer I can use?"

"You have a website?" I asked, reaching for

my laptop. "Aren't you afraid someone's going to steal your designs?"

She shook her head. "The website's public, but my portfolio is in a private section, so only I can access it, but I can share it with people if they sign a privacy agreement."

Katie took the laptop from me and started typing.

"Have you actually needed to make people sign the agreement?" I dared to ask.

She shrugged. "A couple magazines that wanted to interview me."

"A couple . . . Interview?" The words barely made it past my lips.

Katie turned my laptop so I could see the page. "Here we go!"

My mind . . . was blown.

This was the kind of website I dreamed of having in ten years, and Katie had it now. Adorable pop music in the background, a video of her giving fashion tips, links for interviews and podcasts she'd done . . .

In the center of it all was a dress rack that you could hover over to pull out one of her designs and look at. And her designs were good. I had half a mind to take back the top I'd shown her and say, "Kidding! My six-year-old brother made these."

"What do you think?" she asked shyly.

"I think," I said with a nervous smile, "that this town just got a little more interesting."

2

The Amazing Katie Kestler

"A or B? A or B?" Brooke was holding up two pictures, moving one close to my face, then the other, over and over. "Come on, V. Help me pick my costume!"

It was Monday morning before school, and we were sitting in the courtyard, talking about the Schwartzes' upcoming Halloween party.

"Aren't they pretty much the same?" I asked, taking the pictures from her. "They both have the logo of a hairy guy holding a butterfly net."

"That's a lion holding a staff," Brooke said with a frown. "It's for Chelsea FC."

She was talking about Chelsea Football Club, her favorite European soccer team. Brooke is mildly obsessed with the sport. She's the captain of her traveling team, the Berryville Strikers.

"Sorry, a lion, then," I said. "It's still the same outfit."

"But different players." She took back the photos. "How can you not know the difference between Terry and Hazard?"

"I do not know." I shook my head. "But I hate myself every day for it."

Brooke stuck her tongue out at me.

Beside us, Heather snickered. "Why don't you go as Sherlock Holmes?" She nudged Brooke with her toe.

Along with soccer and the newspaper, Brooke's also part of a school group called the Young Sherlocks. They study "the art of deductive reasoning," but I'm pretty sure that means sitting around watching detective shows.

"I would if we were actually doing something," said Brooke. "We've had nothing to investigate this fall."

"The Case of the Boring Autumn," I said.

"Hey!" A pixie-haired girl frowned at me as she walked by.

"Oh, sorry, Autumn! Not you!" I called after her and then winced at my friends. "Whoops."

"She'll get over it," Heather assured me with a pat on the shoulder.

"What are *you* going to your family's party as?" I asked her.

"I won't tell you what it is specifically," she said. "But I will say it's inspired by my Model UN research."

I scrunched my face thoughtfully. Heather was representing Ireland in Model UN.

"Leprechaun is too easy," I said. "Potato?"

Heather cracked up. "What?"

I grinned and shrugged my shoulders. "Those

are the only two things I know about Ireland!"

"Well, I'm going as a person, not a plant," she said with a smile, "which means no four-leaf clover costume, either. You'll have to wait and be surprised."

"Back to *my* costume dilemma," said Brooke, waving the photos in front of my nose. "*A* or *B*?"

"Why do you want to go as a soccer player, anyway?" I asked, moving her arm aside. "You're already a soccer player in real life."

"So?"

"So Halloween is about stepping outside your comfort zone and being something no one would expect," I said. "These?" I pointed to the two photos and shook my head.

"Says the girl who lives outside her comfort zone," said Heather with a smirk.

Brooke pointed to her. "She's right. Every day is Halloween for you."

"No," I said. "Halloween for me will be—"

I stopped when I realized my best friends were leaning forward expectantly. "A surprise."

"Mine will be too," said Brooke.

"Only because you don't even know what you're going to be," I teased.

A shadow loomed over the three of us, and we all craned our necks to look up at Tim.

I don't really go for sporty guys, but I had to admit, all the girls who crushed on him had good taste. He was tall with strong Greek features and a swagger that said he knew it.

"What are you doing at school on time?" asked Brooke. Her eyes widened. "Or are we all really late?" She looked at her phone.

"I'm assistant sports reporter, remember?" he said. "I had to interview one of the football players, and morning practice was the only time he could do it."

"Aw, nice!" said Heather. "So that—"

She paused for a minute while Tim said hi

to a girl strolling past. Brooke and I rolled our eyes. It had been this way since he started working for the advice column. Most girls thought he was funny and smart, which he was, but the way they worshiped him, you'd think he could also turn Payless into Prada.

"Aaand I'm back!" he told Heather.

Heather nodded. "So that position is working out?"

"Eh." Tim waggled his hand from side to side. "The column's great. Rescuing my gym clothes from the bottom of the pool . . . not so much."

"What?!" Brooke, Heather, and I exclaimed at the same time.

"Someone's bullying you?" asked Brooke. "Who is it? I'll . . ."

"Talk to them so I get bullied even more?" Tim finished for her. "You sound just like Gabby."

Gabby was Tim's twin sister, and let's just say I wouldn't want to get on her bad side. Last month, after a guy stood her up on a date, she tried to throw a bucket of grape goo over his head. Luckily, Heather and Brooke were able to stop her and set her back on track, but who's to say what she'd do for family?

"It's really okay," Tim assured us. "The guys just pick on me because of the attention I get from the girls."

"Well," said Heather with an apologetic shrug, "you kind of encourage it."

"I know. I just wish the older guys respected me more as a sports reporter. I'm just as into it as they are."

If a sport had a season, Tim was playing it. From what I'd heard, he was pretty good at baseball. And if his clothes kept winding up at the bottom of the pool, soon he'd be an excellent swimmer too.

"Enough about that. What were you talking about when I came over?" he asked.

"The Halloween party at my house," said Heather. "The prize for this year's costume contest is free movie admission for a month at Cinema Town. They're one of my dad's clients," she added.

Heather's father was an accountant, and since he couldn't keep any gifts his clients offered, he passed them along.

"Free for a month?" Tim repeated. "Consider that prize in the basket for yours truly." He mimed a fadeaway jump shot.

"What are you going as?" asked Heather.

Brooke held up a hand. "Wait! I know this one. Tim is going as one of his fangirls, so he can remind us in third person how great he is."

Heather and I laughed.

"No, I'll be going as someone who none of you will recognize. Because he's from a classic novel."

"Hey, we know the only one that matters: *The Three Musketeers*," said Brooke, grinning at

Heather and me. That had been our nickname since elementary school.

"Oh!" Heather snapped her fingers. "Are you going as the fourth Musketeer? What's his name . . . Darth Vader!"

Tim snapped his fingers back at her. "It's d'Artagnan! And no, but I like that you tried." He pointed to me and Brooke. "You could learn a lot from her."

"Anyway," said Brooke, turning to me. "How was Chicago? Did you get that part for your costume? What was it again?" She blinked innocently at me.

"Nice try," I said. "And yes, I did. Also, I learned that if you lick the window of a nice store, they will ask you to leave."

Tim gave me a strange look. "I'm . . . I'm pretty sure that's true at any store."

"Why were you licking the window?" asked Heather.

"Me?" I stared at her. "Really? I look like a window-licker?"

"It's always the people you least suspect," she said with a solemn headshake, but I saw her elbow Brooke in the side.

"The first step in getting over a window-licking problem is admitting you have a window-licking problem," chimed in Brooke.

I tried to match their serious expressions, but my cheeks started to ache from needing to smile.

"Would you stop?" I finally said with a giggle. "It wasn't me. It was my brother, and he's six."

"Well, it sounds like you had an interesting day," said Heather.

"I did. And . . . an interesting evening."

"How so?" asked Tim.

I'd been debating whether to tell them about Katie since I'd felt a little intimidated by her, but I wanted their opinions.

"We have new neighbors across the street," I

said. "And they have a daughter our age."

"Dark hair, blue eyes, well-dressed?" asked Brooke.

"Yeah," I said, wide-eyed. "Did I tell you about her already?"

"No," Brooke said, pointing. "She's right behind you."

I turned, and sure enough, Katie was strutting toward the building in the cutest blazer-and-jeans combo I had ever seen. She smiled and hurried when she saw me.

"Hey, Vanny!" she called, and waved.

"Vanny?" repeated Brooke.

I shushed her.

"A girl that cute can call Vanessa anything she likes," said Tim out of the corner of his mouth.

I kicked him and waved at Katie.

"Hey, I didn't know you were going here!" I greeted her.

She leaned over and air-kissed me on both

cheeks. "It's the only middle school in the area, silly! Of course I'd go here." Then she turned toward my friends. "I recognize all of you from Vanny's pictures! Brooke, Heather, and Tim, right?" She pointed to each of them in turn. "I'm Katie."

My friends all said hello, Tim adding a handshake to his.

"So you just moved to the area?" asked Heather.

Katie nodded. "From Los Angeles. My dad's textile company just opened a new branch in Chicago, which they can't manage without him, so he whisked us all away." She faced me. "He's actually how I got started in fashion."

"You're into fashion too?" asked Brooke. "I'm surprised Vanessa didn't ask you to live with her."

"Katie's a really good designer," I told them.

"So are you!" said Katie.

"Yes, she is," agreed Heather. "She writes fashion advice for our school paper."

"And I'll bet she's awesome at it," said Katie.

"But not as awesome as Katie!" I blurted. "She's been interviewed in magazines."

What was I doing? My friends were trying to talk me up, and I was passing the praise on to someone else.

"Really?" asked Brooke. "Which magazines?"

Katie waved it away with a dismissive hand. "Nothing big. Just some local stuff, and *Vogue*."

"*Vogue*?" asked Tim. "That's impressive!"

"The article was mainly about my dad," she said, "and they happened to add a little piece about me when they learned I was in a different part of the business."

The school bell rang, and we all looked at one another.

"Well, Brooke and I have to get to homeroom," I said, waving to the others. "Katie, do you know where you're going?"

"I think so," she said. "I'm in Mr. Feldman's class."

"Mine's right by his!" said Heather. "I'll walk with you and show you around."

"Thanks," said Katie with a grateful smile.

"Any friend of Vanessa's is a friend of mine."

"I'll walk with you too," said Tim. "I have . . . something to do near there."

Brooke and I looked at each other and rolled our eyes again.

I held her arm so that we walked slower than the others, and when they'd entered the building, I stopped her.

"What do you think of Katie?" I asked.

Brooke shrugged. "She seems nice enough. Why? Is there something wrong with her? Is she someone's evil twin?" She grabbed my arm. "Is that why her parents really had to move?"

I laughed. "No, she's just . . . very impressive."

"Yeah. You don't think that's cool?" asked Brooke.

To be honest, I wasn't sure what I thought. I guess it was more of how I felt: intimidated, inspired, excited, but mainly . . . worried, for some reason.

"No, it's cool," I said. "Let's go inside."

But we could barely make it through the door before bumping into a crowd.

"What's going on?" asked Brooke, hopping up and down to see over the other kids.

I was a little taller and could already see the cause of the commotion.

"Katie," I said. "Everyone wants to meet the new girl."

"Well, we've already met her." Brooke linked her arm through mine. "Let's try to battle our way through this."

As we plunged into the crowd, I caught snippets of conversation. Some was typical New Kid

Convo: "Where are you from?," "I love California!," and "What neighborhood are you in?"

But there was also: "I love your outfit!," "You design your own clothes? That's cool!," and "Want to go shopping with me sometime?"

There it was again. That worried feeling in the pit of my stomach. I would've stuck around and tried to hear more, but Brooke was practically ripping my arm out of its socket, dragging me down the hall. I supposed I'd hear all the gossip at some point in the day, anyway.

But I was wrong.

I didn't hear the gossip at some point in the day; I heard it all day. It started out as a trickle of information in homeroom.

"So that new girl, Katie, is from Los Angeles. They moved here because of her dad's job."

By midmorning, there was a steady flow of Katie facts.

"She's got her own website. Did you see it?"

"Yeah, and apparently so has Macy's! She actually talked them into looking at her clothes."

And by lunchtime, things had taken a bizarre turn.

"I heard the president of the United States goes to Katie for fashion advice."

"What possible fashion advice could Katie give the president?" I asked my friends.

"'That tie makes you look fat'?" suggested Tim.

"'Red, white, and blue aren't your colors'?" offered Heather.

Brooke didn't respond. She had a sandwich hanging out of her mouth while she texted on her phone.

"Who are you talking to?" I asked, poking her arm.

Brooke's lips moved around the top and bottom of the bread. "Aboo."

"That is the epitome of talking with your

mouth full," said Tim. "What did you say?"

"I think she said 'Abel.'" Heather took the sandwich away from Brooke, minus the chunk trapped between her teeth. "You do know you're going to see him after school?"

Abel Hart was the seventh-grade track star Brooke was dating.

"I know that," she said. "But he thinks he's right about something, and that grave error must be corrected now."

The rest of us exchanged amused looks. Heather says Brooke and Abel have a love-hate relationship. He loves to tease her, and she hates it.

"What's the argument now?" I asked.

"Well, I decided to change my Halloween costume because someone had an issue with it." She looked at me. "And I told him I was going as a hockey player instead. So he said, 'Why don't you go as something cute and girly?'" She lowered her phone. "Has he met me? I am not girly!"

"Love how you don't deny the cute part," said Tim, coughing into his hand and looking away. Brooke threw a baby carrot at him.

"You're still missing the point of Halloween," I said. "You're a tomboy. If you dress like any athlete, nobody's going to be surprised or say 'Great costume.' But if you dress"—I took her carrots away—"cute and girly, people are going to notice."

"But what if he prefers the new cute-and-girly me?" asked Brooke. "I don't think I could care so much about clothing." She shrugged at me. "No offense."

"Then you'll break up with him after the party," said Heather. "But not during. Apparently, that happened last year, and some guy ended up wearing the punch bowl home on his head."

"And you don't have to care about clothes," I

said. "I actually enjoy not hearing someone talk about that for once today. The way everyone's talking, you'd think Katie was Donatella Versace."

My friends stared blankly at me.

I tried again. "Coco Chanel."

"Ooh, I love that it's cold enough for hot cocoa again!" said Heather.

I turned to Tim. "Okay, now I get your frustration when you talk about old books."

"Thank you," he said.

Heather was still caught up in the joys of cold weather. "Also s'mores and hot apple pie and beef stew and baked potatoes . . ."

For a tiny girl, Heather had a massive appetite. Her lunch that day had included a foot-long deli sandwich.

The bell rang, and we headed for Journalism and our desks in the corner. We dropped our bags under our seats while Mrs. Higginbotham, our newspaper adviser, chatted at the front of the room with our student editor in chief, Mary Patrick Stephens.

Mary Patrick is a trip. The very first time I ever saw her outfit, I could tell the kind of person she was. They say clothes make the man (or girl, in this case), and I wholeheartedly agree.

Today, she was wearing khaki slacks with pleats ironed into them, and a crisp, pink, button-up shirt tucked neatly into her pants. Her argyle headband matched her belt and her watch strap. All she was missing was a "Miss Prim 'n' Proper Award" sash.

Mary Patrick glanced in our direction, as if she'd heard my thoughts, and I quickly looked down at my own watch. It definitely didn't match the print scarf in my hair or the silver chain-link belt around the waist of my red jumpsuit.

"Papers are heeeere!" sang Brooke, pointing to the front of the room.

The *Lincoln Log*, our school newspaper that

contained the "Lincoln's Letters" advice column, came out every Monday (which meant staffers turned their work in the previous Friday).

The first few issues had been delivered by the staffers, so people could get to know us, but now the issues just waited by the classroom doors, and the teachers distributed them. It's probably for the best. I ended up with a bad haircut after the first delivery.

Mrs. H still kept some extra copies for her staffers to look at, though, and for us to talk about ways to improve the paper. "Issues with the issue," she called it. Last week, for example, the front page had an article that was all sorts of wrong, and our class got a lecture on fact-checking.

Today's paper was distributed around the room so that each section had a copy. Brooke, as our team leader, was handed ours, but she spread it open on her desk so we could all see.

"Good advice to Beat Feet," Heather told Brooke, tapping the page.

All our advice requesters either use fake names or we assign them fake names to avoid the embarrassment of having everyone know, say, that someone's afraid of getting eaten alive by snails.

"Thanks," said Brooke. "You'd be surprised how many people wear the wrong running shoe for their foot type. Having the right shoes makes a big difference."

"I've got you talking about shoes!" I pretended to sob into my hands. "I have nothing more to teach you."

Brooke, Heather, and Tim laughed.

There was a buzzing sound from the front of the room, and we all looked up to see Mary Patrick with buzzer in hand, standing beside Mrs. H.

"I wonder who's on the chopping block this

week," Heather said in a soft voice.

"Gil, maybe," said Brooke.

We all glanced to our right to look at our assistant photographer/horoscope guru. Tie-dyed T-shirt, cargo pants with patches of rock bands sewn on the knees, and shaggy brown hair in need of styling . . . Gil was a designer's dream makeover project.

"Why Gil?" asked Heather.

"I heard his horoscopes have been way off the mark," said Brooke.

Tim snorted. "Horoscopes are make-believe nonsense. Who cares?"

Since we shared a page with Gil, I glanced up at the horoscope he'd written for my sign, Leo. This week's was in haiku.

A lion roars loud
But don't be surprised this week
If nobody hears

I frowned. "Yeah, horoscopes are dumb."

"Good morning, class!" said Mrs. H. "We've got a lot to do this week with our special Halloween issue coming out next Monday, so let's get started with improvements. Advice column . . ."

Every single person in the class turned to look at us.

"Us?" squeaked Brooke.

Mrs. H nodded. "It appears you've made an enemy out there."

CHAPTER

3

Something to Prove

"What . . . W-who?" sputtered Brooke.

I took the paper from her and reread my previous week's advice to Tank Girl, who wondered what hairstyle went best with her tank top. My advice was still solid, and there was no way it could've produced an enemy, so this wasn't about me.

I relaxed and leaned back to hear Mrs. H's explanation.

"It's not as bad as it sounds," she assured us, "but I thought it was a problem that everyone in the class could help with."

"What happened?" asked Heather.

"Apparently, last month, when Brooke was delivering papers, she talked to a boy named Ryan and told him she knew quite a bit about sports and fitness."

"Well . . . yeah," Brooke said defensively. "That's why I write that portion of the advice column."

Mrs. H nodded. "And I'm not arguing that. But he is. He came to me and asked why you four are the ones who get to give advice, instead of someone like him."

"Because we created the column!" Brooke threw her hands into the air. "If he wanted to give advice so bad, he should've signed up for Journalism."

"And the only reason he even cares is because our column is popular, and he's jealous," I couldn't help adding.

"He doesn't care about the students," chimed

in Heather. "Not like we do."

"We even have our own rule book." Tim held it up.

It was just a sketchbook of mine, but Tim used it to jot down rules we came up with to be better advice columnists.

Mrs. H held up a hand to silence our protests. "You are incredible advice columnists, but he does make a valid argument that I have to address. Which is why I suggested we hold"—she paused dramatically—"an advice-off."

"Ooooh!" said several people.

Brooke leaned back in her chair and crossed her arms. "Fine."

"Brooke!" Up front, Mary Patrick's arms were crossed as well. "We talked about this, remember?"

She meant Brooke's habit of agreeing to *anything* before finding out all the facts. That was how she got so overwhelmed last month.

"Oh, oops." Brooke sat up. "I mean . . . tell me more about the advice-off."

"Mary Patrick and I are still finalizing the rules," said Mrs. H, "but the basic idea is that the four of you—"

"Uh . . . excuse me," I interrupted. "The four of us?"

"Yes, I'd like to see you all participate in this challenge," said Mrs. H. Without pausing for a response, she continued, "The four of you will face off against students in each of your advice areas. If the student wins, they get to give advice in your place for a week."

"Not to mention we look like chumps," Tim muttered, but not quietly enough.

"Then it's in your best interest to give your best advice, isn't it?" asked Mrs. H, arching a brow.

Heather raised her hand. "So Brooke will be

up against this Ryan boy, but what about the rest of us?"

Mrs. H opened her arms wide to the entire class. "That's where all of you come in. Who would you like to see paired up against our esteemed advice columnists?"

It was quiet for a moment, and then people started shouting suggestions.

Mrs. H pointed to Mary Patrick, who grabbed a marker and started scribbling the names on a whiteboard. Most of them were kids I didn't know from higher grades, but there was one who seemed to be on everyone's minds.

"Vanessa Jackson versus Katie Kestler!" someone called out.

I groaned and covered my face with a hand.

"Look, Vanessa's already scared!" someone else said, and everyone laughed.

I quickly lowered my hand and forced a confident smile.

"Bring it," I said, tapping my fingernail on the desk. "I'll prove Katie's not so great-y." I looked to my friends for agreement.

Brooke shook her head. "I'm afraid I can't support bad rhyme."

Mary Patrick circled Katie's name on the board and wrote mine beside it. As soon as everyone was distracted with finding a match for Heather, I dropped the smile and slumped in my chair.

Tim poked me in the side. "You okay?"

I flashed him a thumbs-up. "Couldn't be better."

"You're going to do fine, you know," he said. "Katie's no Vanessa Jackson."

I perked up a little. "You think?"

He nodded. "You'll be great. As long as they don't do a live broadcast of the advice-off."

"Did someone say live broadcast?" Mrs. H asked over the din of conversation. The woman . . . missed . . . nothing. "That's an excellent idea!"

"Whoops. Heh." Tim shifted away from me.

"Wise decision," I said, giving him a tight smile.

Brooke and Heather exchanged worried glances.

"Uh . . . are we sure we want to air this?" asked Brooke.

I knew she was thinking about our last broadcast to introduce the entire newspaper staff. Mrs. H had held a Meet the Press event, during which I'd frozen in front of the camera.

"Please. I'll be fine!" I said with a laugh. "That was a long time ago!"

It was a month ago.

"And it wasn't that bad."

I'm pretty sure I almost wet my pants.

"Besides," I added, "while I've been working on the drama club's costumes, I've been watching them onstage. I think I can handle it."

It took a few more minutes for matches to be found for Heather, who was paired against the school counselor's eighth-grade assistant, and Tim, who was paired against our quarterback.

Mrs. H assured us she'd speak to our advice-off opponents to make sure they were up for it, and then she moved on to discuss business for other sections. When we broke back into our small groups, my friends had varying reactions to the advice-off.

"My competition might be older, but I'm funnier," said Tim, gnawing on the end of his pen and jiggling his legs a million miles an hour. "I ain't scurred."

I smirked at him. "Really? Because your legs look like they're about to run off without you."

Tim took the pen from his mouth long enough

to stick his tongue out at me.

"Well, I'm excited about this," said Heather, eyes shining. "I'd love to know if I give advice that's just as good as someone who counsels kids all the time."

"I am so going to wipe the floor with that Ryan kid," said Brooke. Her eyes were shining too, but more like those really sharp knives you see at a hibachi restaurant.

"Calm down, killer," I said.

"Vanessa, are you sure you're going to be okay with a live broadcast?" asked Heather.

"Yeah, we can ask Mrs. H to keep yours private, if that's easier," said Brooke.

I shook my head. "No, that's silly. I can do this."

Plus, if Katie was brave enough to be on camera, I could not have that be yet another thing she was better at.

"So how do we get ready for this?" I asked.

"Let's start by identifying our weaknesses and coming up with solutions," said Brooke, opening her spiral notebook. "For example, I'm not so great with questions about male fitness, so I'll ask Abel what general concerns guys might have. Who's next?" she asked while she wrote.

"I'm really bad at being sensitive," said Tim. "If someone tells me they're sad about a breakup, my first thought is . . . why?"

"Yikes," said Heather, grimacing. "I figured sensitivity came naturally with all the culture and museums and classic literature you're into."

"Nope," he said, banging on his chest. "My heart is surrounded by barbed wire. Anyway, my solution will be to watch a bunch of rom coms and try to get in touch with my inner nice guy."

Brooke nodded and scribbled in her notebook. "You might want to focus on more relationship questions, too, like . . . how can a girl convince her boyfriend that he's not always right?" She glanced up from her writing. "I'm asking for a friend."

He rolled his eyes. "Does your friend's name rhyme with 'Brooke is a dork'?"

"I don't think anything rhymes with that," said Heather. She put a hand on Brooke's arm. "Is this still about the costume?"

"It's about a lot of things." Brooke put down her pen. "I'm terrible at dating. It feels like Abel and I always fight."

"Because you both have egos and want to be right," said Tim. "But when you're in a couple, you have to let the other person have their way sometimes. Not everything is worth fighting over."

Heather regarded him with wide eyes. "Excellent advice, Barbed Heart!"

Tim grinned, and I nodded in agreement.

"It's like my mom tells her clients when they want everything on their new house wish list but can't have it," I said. "You have to give a little to get a little."

Brooke sighed. "Fine. I'll try and be easier to get along with, as much as it pains me." She returned to her spiral notebook. "Back to the advice-off. What's your weakness, Vanessa?"

"Katie Kestler," supplied Tim.

Brooke and Heather smiled.

I gave Tim a withering look. "Katie's nothing. My weakness is giving advice on hair care products because my hair is so much different from everyone else's. My solution will be to read up on recommendations."

"Great. Heather?" asked Brooke.

"Mine is dealing with angry people," she said. "I think because I don't get mad easily, it's hard to relate. My solution will be to—"

"Hulk out!" cried Tim.

Brooke and I laughed, and Heather shook her

head. "No, to read recommendations for anger management."

"Perfect." Brooke flipped her notebook shut. "While you guys work on this week's advice *and* being kinder, gentler souls with bouncy hair, I'm going to talk to Mrs. H and see if I can't help with the rules of the contest." She gave a sly eyebrow wiggle and then hurried away.

When people have questions for "Lincoln's Letters," they either email them or drop them off in a box outside the classroom. Heather had already fetched the most recent collection and spread them out on her desk.

"What have we got this week?" I asked, sifting through the pile. "Girl who talked behind her friend's back and got caught."

"Mine," said Heather, taking it.

"Girl who accidentally killed her boyfriend's iguana."

"Um . . . maybe mine?" She tried to read the paper upside down. "What's the question?"

"'How attached are guys to their pets?'"

"I'll take that one," said Tim. "And I think this is for you."

He handed me a slip of paper.

"'Dear Lincoln's Letters,'" I read. "'Is plaid played out? I've got a cute plaid skirt I've been meaning to pair with this nautical top I bought.'" I winced. "Oh, honey, no."

"What's wrong with that?" asked Heather.

"Nautical tops usually mean stripes, and stripes look horrible with plaids. Plus, nautical tops tend to have an open neckline, and if you're already showing leg, you need a more modest top."

"Spoken like a future fashion designer," Heather said with a smile.

Heather, Tim, and I sorted through the rest of the pile for more material. Even though we'd each only be answering one question for the paper, the *Lincoln Log* also had a website, where we posted more answers to kids' questions.

Brooke came back just as we were ranking the questions we wanted to answer by priority.

"Okay, here's what we've sorted out so far," she said. "The advice-off will be held over two days, starting next Monday."

"Next Monday?" I repeated, my eyes bugging out. "That's, like, no time to prepare!"

Brooke nodded. "That's the point. We're pretty much facing off with the knowledge we have now. The advice-offs will be broadcast during homeroom, and students will fill in ballots for who they think gave the best answer. Tim and I will go first on Monday, and Heather and V will go Tuesday."

"So we have to get kids to watch us and vote for us," said Tim. "How do we get their interest?"

"With a little help from your sister," Brooke

said with a sly smile. "And Locker 411."

Locker 411 was the invention of Tim's twin sister, Gabby, conveniently located at locker number 411. It started off (after her dismal dating experience) as a mini-library of information that girls might need to survive middle school, but in just one month it had grown to be a resource for all the day's best gossip, too.

"Do people really check that?" he asked dubiously.

"The girls do," said Heather. "They even talk about you."

"Yeah, I think Mia Green wrote *Tim Antonides is a jerk* inside the door," I said.

Tim grinned sheepishly. "That's for something I did with water balloons and fruit punch," he said. "Did you wipe off the note?"

I shrugged. "I thought it was funny, so I didn't even try."

"It's a comfort to know you're on my side."

Tim clapped me on the shoulder. "Is there possibly any good stuff?"

Heather opened her mouth to answer, but Brooke put a hand on her arm.

"Don't tell him. His ego is big enough as it is."

He grinned. "Oh, so there *is* good stuff. I could use it after the drawing someone left on my locker. I'm playing football in a tutu."

Heather giggled and clapped a hand over her mouth.

"Those guys do *not* like you," said Brooke.

"Can I see the drawing?" I asked.

Tim rolled his eyes. "I really struck gold in the friends department."

We all laughed.

"So is everyone okay with the plan?" asked Brooke.

Heather and Tim nodded, and I begrudgingly joined them.

By the end of the day, Locker 411 had already

started to do its job. When I walked into the auditorium after school, the student director of the drama club glanced over at me and beamed.

"Jackson versus Kestler! The most infamous smackdown of the century."

"Hey, Phoebe." I forced a smile and hugged the swatches of fabric I'd brought with me. "I wouldn't call it infamous. It's nothing, really. Not even worth watching."

"Don't be silly," she said. "Of course we'll all watch and support you."

"I'm a lucky, lucky girl," I told her, forcing the smile even wider.

"Oh! And here are the measurements you asked for." Phoebe slid a sheet of paper off her clipboard. "Can you make them work?"

The cast of the play was small, three girls and two guys, but the play itself was set in the distant future, so I'd be making costumes from scratch. The fun part, though, was coming up with the designs and sharing them with the director.

I nodded at the page she gave me. "These are great, thanks! Tell me what you think of these fabrics." I held up each swatch as I described it. Even just talking about fashion lifted my mood. "This is for meeting the aliens, a bit muted and reserved, and this is for the big fight scene, lots of flash and aggressive colors."

Phoebe nodded along to everything I said. "I like them, but can we get something like this one in a less shiny fabric?" She held up a silvery swatch. "I'm worried about the glare from the stage lights."

"Of course," I said with a nod, reaching into my bag. I handed her a hand-stapled lookbook I'd put together. "And I made some form sketches with swatches on them, so you can get an idea of the final product. Obviously, we'll switch out the shiny silver for a matte now."

Phoebe flipped through the lookbook,

smiling. "Awesome! You have got some gift, V. You're totally going to win your advice-off."

I blushed and grinned. "Thank you."

She handed back the book. "Just make that one fabric change, and we're good to go!"

I took the book from her but didn't move.

"Sorry, was there something else?" she asked.

"Actually, I was hoping that after practice I could maybe use the stage?"

Phoebe nodded. "Sure. Is it for anything special? Do you need access to the props room?"

I shook my head. "I just need to practice for the advice-off. I'm a little nervous," I said.

"Someone as poised and confident as you?" She looked surprised. "Just remember to take deep breaths," she added with a smile. "When people get nervous and try to speak, they end up sounding like hyper chipmunks."

I laughed. "Thanks for the tip."

The actors took to the stage, and I listened

and watched while studying their measure-ments and doing more sketches. After an hour, they stopped for a break, and Phoebe approached me.

"We'll be off the stage for about fifteen min-utes if you want to use it," she said.

"That's perfect," I said. "Thanks!"

I waited for everyone to clear the room and, with a self-conscious glance over my shoulder, I hoisted myself onto the stage and got to my feet.

Clearing my throat, I smiled and spoke to an invisible audience, "Hi, I'm Vanessa Jackson and—"

There was a clicking sound from overhead, and suddenly, the stage was awash with light. A girl's voice boomed from above. "You can keep going. I'm just running AV tests."

But I was a Vanessa-deer-in-stage-lights, fro-zen with fear.

"Hello?" her voice boomed again. "I said you

can keep going. Your name is Vanessa Jackson and . . . ?"

"Uhhh. Uhhh." My throat felt like it was lined with crushed crackers. I swallowed and tried again. "Uhhh?"

"I can barely hear you. Use the mic," suggested the voice.

A command. That was helpful. Something to take my mind off the fact that a stranger was watching me and could probably see the sweat rings under my armpits.

I reached for the microphone, but it must've been coated with grease because it slipped out of my hands. I caught it by the cord and tried to swing it back up to grab it, but I misjudged the length of the cord and smacked myself in the head with the microphone. The thud of metal meeting face echoed throughout the auditorium, along with my dry-throated "Uhhh!"

"You okay?" asked the voice.

I nodded and said in a rush, "My name is Vanessa Jackson, and I write fashion and style advice for the *Lincoln Log*."

Phoebe had been right. I sounded like a hyper chipmunk.

I put the microphone back and hopped off the edge of the stage. Clearly, this wasn't something I'd be able to tackle on my own.

I left the auditorium and texted Mom to come get me. Then I dialed a different number.

A minute later, Heather answered my call. "Hey, V, what's up?"

The crackers in my throat had finally crumbled away, and I was able to talk again.

"I have a life-or-death situation," I said. "Can you be at my house in twenty minutes?"

CHAPTER

4

Om My Gosh

" **T**hanks for coming over so quickly," I told Heather when she showed up at my door twenty minutes later.

"You told me it was a life-or-death situation," said Heather, stepping inside. She looked me up and down. "And now that I see you're eating a Popsicle while in your pajamas, it's clear we have different meanings of life and death."

"Sorry." I gripped the Popsicle in my teeth and helped her take off her coat. "I'm trying to give myself brain freeze," I said, talking around a mouthful of ice-cold cherry.

"You *want* brain freeze?" she asked. "Isn't that something most people avoid?"

I shook my head. "I'm hoping if my brain is numb, the rest of me won't be."

Heather regarded me warily. "Maybe we're already past the point of brain freeze." She gingerly took the Popsicle from me. "How many of these have you had, sweetie?"

"Counting this one, which I accidentally dropped in the toilet? One."

"Gahh!" Heather let go of the stick, and the Popsicle splattered onto the tile floor. "V, that's gross!"

"It still had the wrapper on!" I said, picking up the broken pieces. "And the toilet water was clean." I made a face. "Okay, now that I hear myself, you may have a point. But I'm under a lot of stress!"

I carried the pieces into the kitchen, and Heather followed, calling hello to my mom and brother in the living room.

"What's going on?" Heather asked while I tossed the Popsicle bits into the sink and washed my hands.

I explained how I'd gotten onstage and frozen in the spotlight, along with giving myself a microphone-shaped bruise.

"Aww." Heather eyed my forehead. "I thought you'd gotten over that fear."

"Yeah, well, apparently, my brain forgot to tell the rest of me." I dried my hands on a paper towel and crumpled it into a ball. "Anyway, you're in front of an audience all the time for choir, so I thought you could help."

Heather was a crazy good singer. Whenever Brooke and I have karaoke at our slumber parties, Heather somehow mysteriously signs up for songs in handwriting that looks nothing like hers.

"Well, I am onstage a lot," she said, "but never by myself."

"You also did great at last month's Meet the Press," I said. "Remember, when we all had to do on-camera segments?"

"True," she said. "But that was just facing a camera, not people."

"I can't even do *that*," I said. "We have the advice-off next week, and I'm going to choke."

"Well, let's see if we can fix that," said Heather with an encouraging smile. "Can we sit someplace more . . . stable?"

She eyed the stool underneath me.

I was pretty sure she meant to say, "Can you sit someplace more stable?," but Heather was the kind of girl who was too sweet to point those things out.

"Sure." I motioned for her to follow, pausing in the living room. "Mom, Heather and I are going to be in my room."

"Can I come?" asked Terrell. "We can all play Battle the Mermaid."

"How about Battle the Paper Towel?" I asked, lobbing it at him.

"Heather, while you're here, are you possibly free on Wednesday afternoon?" asked Mom. "I need someone to watch Terrell while I take Vanessa to the dentist."

Heather winced. "Oh, sorry, Mrs. Jackson, but I have Hebrew school. Maybe Katie could do it? She told me she used to babysit in Los Angeles."

"I'm not a baby!" Terrell gave Heather a defiant stare, and she smiled.

"Excuse me. Young *man*—sit," she said.

"That isn't a bad idea," said Mom.

"We'll ask her tomorrow," said Heather.

"Thank you!" said Mom. "You girls have fun."

I led the way to my bedroom and closed the door.

"Okay, what's the plan?" I asked.

Heather's eyes traveled from me to my closet.

"Actually, I've changed my mind. I'll help you, but it's going to cost."

"You want to borrow one of my outfits? Sure," I said with a shrug.

"Nooo." Heather held up a finger and grinned mischievously. "I'll only help if I can see your Halloween costume *today*."

"My . . ." It was such a devious request from such an angelic face that I couldn't help smiling. "Fine, but you also have to show me what *your* costume is."

"Deal!" said Heather. "Let's see yours first."

I giggled with excitement. Even though I'd wanted to keep my costume a surprise, it was kind of cool to get to show someone.

I walked into my closet and reached into my rack of winter clothes, pulling out my most amazing creation to date.

"Voilà!" I spun it on its hanger so she could see the front and back. "Steampunk princess."

Heather's expression was completely worth it. "That ... is ... awesome."

The skirt was white-and-brown-striped, satiny, and gathered to knee-level at the front. Around the waist of the skirt, I'd swapped fabric for dark-brown leather that I'd accented with copper-colored buttons shaped like gears. For my upper body, I had a white blouse with puffy sleeves under a red textured bodice that had buckles instead of laces.

"V, it's gorgeous!" Heather whispered, running her hands over the material. "You made all this?"

"Well, not the metal pieces," I said with a grin. "But yeah."

"And these gear buttons are adorable!" she raved.

"Thanks. But here's my favorite part." I pointed to the choker around the neck of the hanger. It was red velvet, with the red-and-white cameo dangling from the center. "It belonged to my grandma."

"I bow to the queen of all costumes." Heather bent at the waist.

"Steampunk princess," I corrected her, laughing. "And thank you." I hung the costume on the back of my door. "Okay, your turn. What are you going as?"

Heather searched through the photos on her phone for a minute and then showed me.

"An Irish folk dancer."

"So cute!" I said, taking the phone from her. "I didn't know you could dance like that."

"I can't," she said. "I've been watching some videos online, but they move too fast for me." She took back her phone. "But that's okay because all eyes will be on you, anyway!"

At the mention of all eyes on me, my thoughts

jerked back to the advice-off, and my stomach lurched.

"Can we work on my stage fright now?" I asked.

Heather nodded. "Of course."

She sat cross-legged on the floor and had me do the same.

"We'll start with a breathing exercise," she said. "Breathing is very important when you speak." She paused. "Also for life in general."

She cleared her throat. "This breathing technique is called 'sama vritti,' or 'equal breathing.' You're going to inhale for four counts and then exhale for four counts. Ready?"

I nodded. "I've been breathing my whole life. This'll be easy."

While I talked, Heather took the thumb and forefinger of my left hand and brought them together to form an O. Then she did the same with my right.

"These hand positions guide your energy flow so that you gain wisdom and feel calm." At a strange look from me, she blushed and added, "I sometimes go to yoga with my *bubbe*. Studying stresses me out, and the yoga helps me relax."

I grinned at her. "That's cute that you and your grandma do that together. My grandma drags me to church bingo."

Heather placed her hands on my shoulders. "Now, you're going to take some calming breaths while I count to four. Inhale."

I breathed in, and Heather counted.

"One . . ."

I started to cough.

She stared at me, wide-eyed. "Really?"

I waved away her concern with one hand and stifled my cough with the other.

"I'm fine," I said. "The cold of the Popsicle is still in my throat, I think. Start over."

"Inhale," she said again, counting on her fingers.

I took a deep breath and gave her a triumphant smile.

"Exhale," she said.

I blew a gust of air in her face. She blinked and leaned back.

"Okay, that was supposed to be slowly"—she twitched her nose—"and without the scent of cherries and garlic."

"Sorry, I had pizza for lunch," I said, covering my mouth.

"But you got further this time!" She patted my knee. "Let's try it again. And remember, inhale and exhale slowly. And when you exhale, I want you to say *om* and really feel the vibration." She demonstrated.

We practiced the breathing technique a few more times until I was as calm as I was ever going to be.

"Good," said Heather. "Now it's time for a visualization exercise. If you think it, you can make it."

I gave her a dubious look. "Terrell sometimes thinks he's a dinosaur."

"Just close your eyes." She reached out and placed a hand over them.

"Your palm is sticky," I informed her.

"That's from your toilet Popsicle," she said. "Close your eyes."

I did as she said, and she pulled her hand away. A second later, I heard muted harp music, no doubt from her phone.

"I want you to imagine yourself back onstage," she said. "The spotlights are on, and you're the only one there."

"What am I wearing?"

The music stopped. "Huh?"

"Onstage." I turned my head in her general direction. "What am I wearing?"

"Oh. Um . . . purple pants and a green tank top."

I made a face. "I look like an eggplant."

"I meant blue jeans," she corrected herself, starting the music again.

I wrinkled my forehead. "Boot cut, flared, or skinny?"

The music stopped.

"What?"

"What kind of jeans?" I asked.

"Flared."

"I don't own flared jeans," I said. "When did I buy them?"

Heather sighed. "I don't know. There was a sale at Blarneys?"

"I think you mean Barneys," I said. "And even on sale their jeans are not cheap. Where did I get the money? I didn't babysit those terrible Thatcher boys again, did I?"

I felt Heather's hands clutching both sides of

my head. "You got the money as a birthday present, the jeans were on clearance because they had a stain, and before you ask, you're wearing ballet flats."

I was quiet for a moment. Then I peeked through one eye and asked, "What color are the flats?"

"Vanessa!" Heather squeezed my head, and we both busted out laughing.

After we'd calmed down, I said, "Look, I'm sorry, and I appreciate your help, but visualizing myself confident before an audience won't work. Trust me, I have a constant daydream where I'm holding a fashion show, and"—I shrugged—"that hasn't worked, either."

She shook her head. "I just don't get it. You love being the center of attention, and the spotlight is perfect for that. Even if you're not comfortable in front of two hundred people, you should be okay in front of one camera." She snapped her fingers.

"Remember when we helped Brooke film that video for history? You were in front of a camera then!"

"A cell phone camera," I reminded her. "And I didn't have to look directly at it, and my professional career wasn't at stake!"

"Well—"

Someone knocked on my bedroom door.

"Come in, Mom!" I called.

Only it wasn't my mom. Or my little brother. Or Brooke or Tim Antonides or even Tim Gunn.

"Hiyee!" said Katie, waving to me. "Your mom said I'd find you here, and she asked me to babysit your brother, which of course I said yes to because how cute is he, and plus, you and I are like sisters from different misters, so he's almost family!" She took a deep breath. "But what are you doing by yourself, lonely pants?" She started to walk in and saw Heather off to the side. "Oh! Hi, Heather! Sorry. I just wanted to talk to

Vanny about the advice-off."

"That's actually what we're practicing for," said Heather. "V has a little stage fright."

"Hey!" I turned on Heather with wide eyes. "Why would you reveal my weakness to the competition?"

"Awww, it's okay," said Katie. "My lips are sealed." She pantomimed zipping them shut. "Want me to email you some Toastmasters videos my mom has?"

I was about to point out that she technically wouldn't be able to talk if her lips were really sealed, but her question intrigued me.

"Toastmasters?" I repeated. "What's that?"

"It's a public-speaking improvement group. My mom used to have a serious phobia about speaking in public, so her doctor recommended she join. After a few months—"

"A few months? I only have a week." I looked to Heather to back me up, but she shrugged.

"It couldn't hurt," she said.

Why was she siding with Katie?

"Fine." I nodded at Katie. "Can you email me the files?"

"Sure, give me your business card."

I froze in the process of getting a pen and Post-it. "My what?"

"Business card," she repeated as she reached into her purse and pulled out a flat, pink card case with a black *K* in the center of it. She flipped it open and passed cards to me and Heather.

Of course.

"Wow!" said Heather with the same enthusiasm she'd had for my costume. "These are really nice. And so professional!"

"Awww, thanks!" said Katie. "I want people to take me seriously."

I glanced at the card she'd given me, which I had to admit did look really nice. Her name, her email address, and *Fashion Guru* were written in swirly script meant to look like thread coming off a spool at one end of the card.

"What do you think?" Katie asked me.

"It's great," I said with a tight smile. I wrote my email address on a Post-it and handed it to her. "I don't have business cards yet."

"Oh, Vanny." Katie clicked her tongue. "That just won't do! We'll get on that this weekend."

"Yay!" I said, waving a fist that to her probably looked excited but was really holding back some serious rage. "You said you wanted to see me about the advice-off?"

"Yes!" Katie gripped my arms and set me down on the bed. "Only . . . can we talk in private?"

I glanced at Heather, one of my dearest, closest, lifelong friends, and sent her a telepathic message: *Do not leave me alone with this girl!*

Heather smiled at us and grabbed her bag. "I'll leave you two alone."

Clearly, I could cross off *mental bond* from my

list of best-friend benefits.

As soon as Heather walked out and closed my bedroom door, Katie gasped and put a hand to her chest.

"What's wrong?" I asked. "Are you having a heart attack? Do we need to cancel the advice-off?"

"Vanny, what is this piece of gorgeousness?" She reached for the costume on the back of my door.

"Oh no!" I got to it before she could and then tucked it back into my closet. "Nobody was supposed to see that!"

"Are you kidding? Everybody should see it!" she exclaimed, chasing after me.

I paused and blushed. I had to hand it to Katie. She was an expert at flattery.

"Well, thanks, but it's a surprise for the Schwartzes' Halloween party."

"Gotcha," she said with a wink. "My lips are double sealed."

I sighed and sat on my bed. "I hope so. Now, what did you want to say about the advice-off?"

"Oh, not much." Katie twirled her hair dully. "Except . . ." She clapped her hands against my legs. "Vanny! We are going to own it!"

I cocked my head, not remotely as enthused. "You realize we're competing against each other."

"Yeah, yeah," she said with a dismissive wave. "But we're also competing against everyone else in the advice-off for ratings!"

"Ratings?" I repeated. "This isn't network TV, Katie. It's going to air in every homeroom. People won't have a choice but to watch us."

"Ummm." Katie made a sassy face. "That's so not true. The TVs have to be broadcasting us, yes, but the kids in the classroom don't have to watch."

"Good!" I said. "The less the better! Or have you already forgotten? Stage fright?" I gestured to myself.

"Yes, but you'll get over it," she said. "This is our chance to make a name for ourselves."

"I already have a name," I said. "It's Va*nessa*." I emphasized the ending.

"Vanny!" Katie rolled her eyes, completely oblivious. "You don't take your career seriously enough. No website, no business cards, no drive to be in the public eye."

"I'm twelve," I pointed out. "I'll have plenty of time to get in the public eye later."

"But why not start now? Can't you see the headline?" Katie stood and held her hands open above her head. "'Vanessa Jenkins: Middle-School Millionaire.'"

"It's Vanessa Jackson," I said.

"Oops! Sorry, but if you had a business card, I would've already known that," said Katie, lowering her hands. "Just leave the particulars to me, and we will be the most talked-about girls in school."

"But—"

"Oh!" She glanced down at a pocket watch hanging from her belt loop. "I've gotta jet, because speaking of costumes, I need to find what *I'm* going to wear to the Halloween party. I'll send you those videos tonight! Kisses!"

And in a flash of fabric, she was out the door.

"Wha—"

I wasn't sure what threw me more: that she was also going to the Schwartzes' party, no doubt in a costume that would trump mine, or that she was somehow going to magically make us the most talked-about girls in school.

What exactly was her plan?

CHAPTER

5

Winners and Losers

On Wednesday morning I got to see Katie's master plan in action. But before I even saw it, I heard it.

I was a block from school when I realized the usual chattering and shouting from the front courtyard sounded a little different.

Pop! Laughter. Nervous squeal. *Pop! Pop!* More laughter.

I walked as fast as my houndstooth rain boots would allow, my footsteps drowned out by more popping and squealing and laughter.

When I rounded the corner, the campus was

filled with kids and balloons. Giant rubbery bubbles covered every inch of ground space. And the happiness was contagious.

Above the noise I heard someone call my name. I spotted Brooke and Heather, sitting on the edge of the school fountain and watching the mayhem. They waved to me and I hurried to join them. "What the heck is going on?" I asked with a laugh.

"Are you having fun watching people stomp on you?" asked Brooke.

Heather giggled.

My smile shifted down. "Huh?"

She pointed to Heather, who thrust one of the balloons out in front of her.

"Vanessa Jackson, meet Vanessa Jackson!"

The balloon had my face on it. I don't know why I hadn't noticed earlier. Probably because up until now, my face had only ever been imprinted on sliding glass doors when I ran into them.

"Whoa." I took the balloon from Heather.

"But wait, there's more!" she said in an excited whisper. She reached behind her back and produced a second balloon. This one had Katie's face on it.

"I don't get it," I said, turning the balloons over.

"Apparently, inside one of these balloons is a white ribbon," said Brooke. "Whoever finds the white ribbon gets two free tickets to House of Horror."

"*This* is how she's going to make us famous?" I squeezed the Katie balloon between my fingers, watching her screen-printed eyes bug out until her face exploded.

I'm not gonna lie; it was incredibly satisfying.

"No instant winner here," I said, checking the balloon remains around me.

"I don't think you'd be eligible, anyway," said Brooke. "Since you're also running the contest."

I raised a brow. "I'm what now?"

She handed me a flyer.

"Oh she did not" was all I could say.

There was Katie's face and mine again, this time with the word *Versus* in between them, and *Showdown of the Century!* written across the top.

Underneath our faces in smaller print were the words *Win All Week!*, with various contests, including the balloon pop, that kids could participate in before the big showdown.

Then beneath that in even tinier print was *Brought to you by Katie Kestler and Vanessa Jackson.*

"Well, at least she got my name right," I muttered.

"It's actually pretty clever," said Brooke. "I wish I'd thought of it, although nobody probably cares about my opponent." She made a face. "But Katie's got style!" She clapped me on the back. "Well done!"

"Oh, you say that now," I said, crumpling up the flyer. "But as soon as Mary Patrick and Mrs. H hear about this, I'm sure we'll get another lecture."

Last month, Heather, Tim, and I might have gotten carried away in our new roles as advice columnists. I'd assumed the persona of Van Jackson, fashion-guru extraordinaire, and they'd been my assistants. Poor, sane Brooke had been taken down with us.

"Oh, *we* won't get one." Brooke motioned to herself and Heather, smiling.

"Who won't get what from who?" Katie popped up next to me and bounced her hip against mine. "Hey, girlfriend! Loving the boots-and-tights combo. And you two"—she pointed to Brooke and Heather—"you keep doing you. I love it."

Brooke and Heather grinned at her and then at each other.

I threw up in my mouth a little.

"I was just telling my friends," I said to Katie, "that the last time we tried to increase our publicity, we wound up in big trouble with our Journalism teacher."

Katie looked affronted. "Well, if that happens, you tell her I cleared it with James!"

"James?" I repeated.

"You know, James Winslow . . . the principal?"

"You call him by his first name?" asked Brooke.

Katie shrugged. "He and my mom have been friends since the dawn of the dinosaurs. He knows me and he adores me. We are most def on a first-name basis."

"Of course you are," I said. At this point, Katie could say she was president of the moon and I wouldn't be surprised. "Well, if James is okay with it."

Katie nodded. "As long as we clean up the mess afterward. Which we volunteered to do."

I gritted my teeth. "How thoughtful of us." All around my feet was a sea of balloon bits. "Your parents refuse to use plastic forks, but they're okay with this?"

"These are made from recycled materials!" She gave my arm a swat.

Brooke sidled up to Katie. "Give us a hint. Which balloon has the ribbon?"

"That'd be more than a hint!" Katie said with a laugh. "But I will tell you"—she leaned forward conspiratorially—"you can hear it rattling inside the balloon."

Brooke's eyes widened. "I'm off to shake some balloons!" She gestured to me. "Come on, V! I'll split the prize with you."

I wasn't really interested in the haunted house, but I liked popping balloons, so I started to follow her . . . until I caught a snippet of conversation between Heather and Katie.

"By the way," Katie told Heather, "I talked to

my mom, and you're in."

Heather gasped and pressed her hands together. "You are awesome."

I paused and turned back. "In where?" I asked.

Heather and Katie exchanged a secretive grin.

"So Katie and I were talking on the way to homeroom Monday about my costume for Halloween," said Heather, "and I told her how I've been failing at YouTube dance videos. As it turns out, Katie's mom knows a woman who teaches all kinds of dance, including . . ." She left it open for me to finish.

"Irish folk dancing?" I guessed.

"Yes! And she's going to let me go to some classes."

"That's pretty cool," I admitted.

Maybe Katie wasn't as bad as I thought. Maybe she was just a sweet girl. Maybe—

"And I offered to make Heather's costume," added Katie.

Maybe she was the worst.

I know it wasn't logical, but instantly my jealousy reflex kicked in.

"*She's* helping you?" I asked Heather.

Of all my friends, Heather was the most sensitive and thoughtful, but instead of coming to me, one of her best friends since kindergarten, she was going to a stranger for fashion advice? It felt like a punch to the throat.

"Why didn't you ask me?" I managed to squeak.

Heather at least had the decency to look guilty. "Aw, V, I'm sorry. I would've, but you already seemed really stressed out."

"I'm sorry too, Vanny," chimed in Katie. "If I'd known you'd get upset—"

"Upset? I'm not upset. What makes you think I'm upset?"

Heather cleared her throat. "Well, your nostrils—"

I fixed her with a stare.

"Look so great today!" she finished.

"And I wasn't too stressed to make *this* last night," I said, rolling back my coat sleeve to reveal my sweater sleeve underneath. The cuffs were delicately patterned lace that I'd hand-sewn onto my cashmere hoodie. Sporty *and* sweet.

"Ooh, I love this," said Heather, running her fingers over the fabric. She pushed back my sleeve and looked at my watch. "Yikes! I'm supposed to be in the choir room. Katie, you want to come with me and we'll talk?"

"Sure!" She waved to me. "Later, Vanny!"

"Bye, V!" Heather waved too and hustled away with Katie.

I watched them go, serious wrinkles plaguing my forehead, and wandered over to join Brooke. She was shaking a red balloon like it was a wrapped Christmas present.

"What took you so long?" she asked.

I told her about Heather going to Katie for help, but Brooke's only response was to drop the balloon she was holding and pick up a purple one.

"Well? What do you think of that?" I prompted.

Brooke paused and then shrugged. "I guess it's nice of Katie to help, especially since she just moved here. She's probably doing it to make friends."

"You think?" I bent and picked up a balloon, giving it a slight jiggle. Nothing.

Brooke, meanwhile, shook her balloon for all she was worth. "Why else? To sabotage Heather's costume?" She gasped dramatically and clutched my arm. "Oh no! She's adding sequins!"

"Hilarious." I rubbed the balloon I was holding against Brooke's head until her bangs stood straight up. "Nope. Static is not in fashion this season."

"Like I care," she said with a snort, but then she reached up to smooth her hair. "Listen, why are you so worried about what Katie's doing?"

"She's my competition," I said. "I need to be watching her every move, like a—"

"Stalker?" Brooke supplied.

"Like a hawk," I said, narrowing my eyes at her. "You're not the least bit worried about that Ryan kid?"

"No, and I'll tell you why." Brooke flicked her balloon aside. "I'm meeting with someone special about this. In fact, you can join me, if you want. Heather and Tim too."

"Join you?" I shot her a dubious look. "Is this a cult? Because those people don't dress well."

Brooke raised an eyebrow. "It's not, but good to know the dress code is what's holding you back."

The morning bell rang, and Brooke and I joined the rest of the kids heading into the building. All around us there were still occasional balloon bangs.

"Anyway, who's this someone special?" I asked.

"You know my neighbor Miss Lillian?"

"The woman with the prizewinning show dog? Sure."

"Well, before she showed dogs, she showed people." Brooke let that sink in and then grinned at the confused look on my face. "She was a beauty pageant coach."

I shook my head. "Still lost. We're not competing in a beauty pageant."

"No, but beauty pageant contestants need confidence and stage presence, and they have to have the best answers to questions. Some of them might even have stage fright." Brooke leaned in and held her arms open, waiting for my reaction.

"Oooh." I smiled. "Brilliant! Yeah, definitely count me in."

"Great! I'm meeting with her tomorrow after

school. I'll talk to Heather and Tim and see if they want to come."

"Heather probably will, but Tim . . ." I trailed off. "You might not want to mention that he's learning the same skills as Miss Illinois."

Brooke tapped her chin thoughtfully. "I'll come up with something to tell him."

It took her all morning to think of the perfect idea, and in my opinion . . . she probably should've spent another day or two on it.

"Your neighbor coached guys for the Mr. Classy contest?" Tim wrinkled his nose. "Is that even a real thing?"

Tim, Brooke, and I were sitting in Journalism, waiting for Heather to join us.

"Mr. Classy? You've never heard of it?" Brooke elbowed me. "Tim's never heard of Mr. Classy. It's only the most elite contest for sophisticated gentlemen! They hold it at a museum, for crying out loud."

"How do they pick a winner?" asked Tim.

"What makes a guy Mr. Classy, you ask?" Brooke gazed dramatically into the distance. "He's cultured, suave, stylish . . ."

"So Abel's out," Tim said with a snort.

Brooke glared at him. "Hey! He may not be cultured or suave or stylish . . ." She paused. "Oh yeah, I guess he's out."

"But he's smart," I said. "He should be in our grade, but he got to skip one. And he's well-read, and he started Young Sherlocks."

"Yes, there's that!" She pointed to me. "And I should've said it myself, huh?" She smacked herself on the forehead. "So bad at this dating stuff."

"I think you're being too hard on yourself," I said. "This is strange new territory for you."

She smirked. "You make it sound like I'm an explorer."

"Yeah, like Captain Nemo." Tim snorted. "Am I right?"

Brooke and I exchanged a mystified look.

"*Twenty Thousand Leagues Under the Sea?*" Tim leaned forward. "Seriously? Jules Verne?"

"Ahhh. An old-book thing," Brooke mumbled. "No, I tried what you guys said, meeting Abel halfway on stuff, and it worked."

"Oookay," I said with a chuckle. "Shouldn't that be a good thing?"

"Yeah, he was really happy, but then he asked if I wanted to go to the Halloween party in themed couple's costumes."

"Awww, cute!" I said.

"And we started fighting about *that*," she said. "He wants Bonnie and Clyde, I want Mario and Luigi."

"The Super Mario Brothers?" Tim asked with a grin.

"Yes, because we'll be Italian, and then I can carry around a pizza," said Brooke.

Pepperoni pizza is her favorite food. It figures

she'd let her stomach do the thinking.

"He didn't appreciate your logic?" I asked, giving Tim a wink.

"He still wants me to be something girly," Brooke said with a groan. "I offered to be *Maria* and Luigi, but then he said I was just being ridiculous." She laid her head on her desk.

"Oh, to have problems like yours," I said, patting her hair.

"Uh-oh, what's going on?" asked Heather, dropping her book bag by her desk.

"Brooke wants to be an Italian plumber, but Abel won't let her," Tim explained.

Heather tilted her head to one side, brow furrowed. "I honestly don't have a response for that."

Brooke, Tim, and I laughed.

"It's nothing," Brooke assured her. "Just more dating stuff. Did you get my note about tomorrow after school?"

"At Miss Lillian's?" Heather gave her a thumbs-up. "I'm in!"

Tim turned to her. "Was Miss Lillian really a coach for the Mr. Classy contest?"

Heather burst into giggles. "Mr. what?"

Tim crossed his arms and glowered at Brooke. "I knew you were bluffing."

"But you were hoping I wasn't." She smiled and poked him with her pencil. "Admit it. You kind of wanted it to be real."

"I won't admit it, and I couldn't come tomorrow, anyway," he told her. "I already have other plans. Plus, I don't need any training on how to be awesome. I already am."

"Fine, Mr. Awesome." Brooke leaned back in her chair. "Let's hear the awesome submission you plan to turn in on Friday."

"You think I'm not ready"—Tim reached into his book bag—"but I call your bluff!" He whipped out a sheet of paper and cleared his throat loudly.

"'Dear Lincoln's Letters, I'm new to dating, and my boyfriend and I fight about everything. How can we make—'"

Brooke snatched the letter out of his hand. "This is your handwriting. Where's the original advice request?"

"There isn't one," said Tim. "I thought your issue with Abel was perfect for this because it shows I'm compassionate and care about relationships. Hey! Don't do that!"

He tried to stop Brooke from crumpling the paper, but she twisted out of his reach.

"New rule for the book," she said. "No airing our own dirty laundry in the column."

"Oh, come on!" said Tim. "I have actual proof that the advice works!" He pointed to her.

"I'm with Brooke on this one," I said. "Especially if there's a chance Abel might find out."

Brooke flashed me a grateful smile. "And a rule to follow that: no making up advice requests. We have too many real people who need our help."

"Fine," Tim grumbled, and reached into his bag again, pulling out the rule book.

"How many are we up to?" I asked.

"We just passed number thirteen: don't offer advice that poses a threat." He paused with pen at the ready. "To be fair, when I told that kid to skateboard through a basketball game, I was kidding."

"Yeah, but that didn't stop two of the players from crashing into him," said Brooke.

"Or keep him from getting suspended," added Heather.

I shook my head. "Some guys will do anything to get a girl's attention."

While Tim wrote the two new rules, Brooke turned to Heather. "Do you have your piece for the paper picked out?"

"Yes, and don't forget, I need your web content by Friday." She pointed to all of us.

"Yes, ma'am!" I said, saluting her.

"I'll have it for you by Friday morning." Brooke crossed her heart.

Heather nodded. "Tim?"

He glanced up with a sheepish expression. "I'm . . . going to have to redo all my web content. Unless we can revoke the two new rules we just created."

"You wrote all your advice pieces about me and Abel?" Brooke squeaked, hugging her arms over her chest. "That's my private life!"

"Geez, get over yourself." He rolled his eyes. "It wasn't all about you. I used Heather and Vanessa as examples, too."

"Hey!" Heather and I said.

Tim shielded himself with his hands. "I said I'll redo it!"

"I'm afraid to even ask how you used me as an example." Heather gave him a wary look but picked up her notebook. "Anyway, my advice this week goes to Left Behind, who's a sixth grader like us and seems to have lost most of her friends since coming to middle school."

"Awww. What happened to them?" asked Brooke.

Heather shrugged. "She says they seem to be growing up faster than her and don't hang out as much anymore."

"That's so sad! I would die if I lost you guys." I gripped Brooke's and Heather's arms.

"Hey!" Tim said this time.

"I meant you, too," I told him. "I just don't have a third arm."

The others laughed.

"I've got you covered," said Heather, reaching out and placing a hand on Tim's shoulder. "Anyway," she said for a second time, "here's my response: 'Dear Left Behind, I'm sorry you and your friends are drifting apart. Try telling them how you feel, and don't forget the exciting part of any new school: new people! Don't view all these faces as the faces of strangers. View them as potential friends. You might find you have something in common with one of them that you didn't have with anyone else. So, talk to your old friends but also try talking to some new ones. Confidentially yours, Heather.'"

"Love it!" cheered Brooke while Tim and I clapped.

Heather blushed and smiled. "Thanks, guys. Brooke, what piece do you have?"

She pulled out a slip of paper. "Well, I haven't written out the answer yet, but the question is about healthy snack alternatives."

"'Dear Reader,'" said Tim, posing as Brooke. "'Instead of a whole pepperoni pizza, try half!'"

The rest of us laughed.

"For your information," said Brooke, "I was going to suggest granola bars instead of candy bars, and real fruit Popsicles instead of ice cream.

Also, when you're craving something crunchy, veggies and hummus work just as well as potato chips and dip."

Heather rubbed her stomach. "I know we just ate lunch, but I'm getting hungry again."

More laughter.

"Vanessa, what do you have for us?" asked Brooke.

"I thought I'd do something a little different this time," I said, laying the paper with my advice on my desk so they could all see. "A girl asked about different ways to wear a scarf, so I explained and drew a couple illustrations."

"Clever!" said Brooke.

"Yeah, I'm not so great at drawing the neck area, though," I said, making a face. "Most of my designs are for headless people."

"You know who could probably help with that? Gil," said Tim. "He does the illustrations that go with his column."

"Oh, that's a good idea." I turned in my seat and spotted Gil, who was studying some images on his camera with Stefan Marshall, our lead photographer. "Gil? Could you come here for a sec, please?"

He glanced over at us and smiled a huge dimply grin. "You read my mind! I actually needed to take your photos."

"Our photos?" asked Brooke as Gil walked over.

"Yeah, for a piece we're going to run on next week's advice-off." He held up his camera and pointed it at Brooke. "Say *cheese!*"

"Say *a healthier alternative!*" chimed in Tim.

Brooke burst out laughing just as Gil snapped her picture.

"Sorry, sorry," Brooke said, giggling. "Let me try again."

"Well, let's see if the photo's salvageable," said Gil, looking at the preview window.

There was Brooke, a squinty-eyed blur. We all started laughing.

Stefan strolled over wearing an amused smile. "What's so funny?"

Heather instantly stopped laughing and gazed at him in wonder. She may have a teeny-tiny crush on him.

"Gil is taking our photos for the paper," I supplied.

Stefan turned the camera so he could view the image, and the corner of his lip curled. "Oh, Gil, dude, we can do way better than that."

"Oh, I know," said Gil. "Brooke just—"

"May I?" Stefan took the camera from him and focused on Heather, who was sitting closest. "Come on, Heather. Let's see that dazzling smile."

Heather glowed brighter than the sun.

"Perfect!" He took the shot. "Tim, show me what a real guy is all about."

I expected Tim to roll his eyes and make a silly pose, but he sat tall and tilted his chin up, no nonsense.

Click! Stefan moved on. "Brooke, sporty yet sweet, make it happen!"

This time, Brooke didn't laugh but laced her hands in front of her and grinned.

Click! Stefan turned to me. "Vanessa, where's your inner diva?"

Now, I wanted to roll my eyes, but instead I gave the camera a knowing smirk.

Click! Stefan passed the camera to Gil. "There you go, bro. Catch you guys later!"

"Later!" Heather called after him in a soft voice. When she turned back to us, she was glowing again. "Isn't he great?"

"Yeah, awesome." I glanced at Gil. His dimples had vanished, and he was clutching the camera against him. "Hey, Gil, can we preview those?"

"Uh . . . sure." He held the camera out so we could see. All my friends marveled over the images, but to me, they were just okay.

"What do you think?" asked Gil.

I shrugged. "They'll do, I guess. Listen, can you help me with something?"

"Are you sure Stefan wouldn't do a better job?" he asked with a half smile.

"No." I looked him in the eye. "I don't want his help. I want someone who has talent to help me."

And just like that, the dimples reappeared.

6

No Big Deal

On Thursday afternoon, Brooke's mom picked up her, Heather, and me from school and dropped us off at Miss Lillian's. As soon as Brooke rang the doorbell, there was the scuttle of tiny paws and a whining bark on the other side of the door.

"Hi, Rocket!" Brooke spoke through the door to Miss Lillian's bull terrier, who whined some more.

"Who's here to see us?" I could hear Miss Lillian ask Rocket in a baby voice. She unlatched the door and smiled at me and my friends. "Come in, girls, come in! Let me take your coats." She held out her arms, and we weighed them down with our jackets. "Would you like a snack before we get started? I've got pumpkin muffins and hot chocolate."

Brooke's eyes lit up. "Of course!"

So much for healthy alternatives.

As we sat in Miss Lillian's living room with our muffins and cocoa, she explained the basics of successful showmanship.

"Confidence is key," she said, pacing in front of us. "Even if you don't know an answer, you hold your head high, look the interviewer in the eye, and fake it the best you know how." She stopped in front of Brooke. "Ask me something about soccer, dear."

Brooke chewed her muffin and thought. "What's a red flag?"

Miss Lillian looked Brooke in the eye. "Oh, a red flag is a terrible thing. A player wants to avoid seeing a red flag at all costs."

Brooke smiled. "That's pretty good!"

"Note that while I know nothing about red flags related to soccer, I know enough about the *symbol* of a red flag to know it's a bad thing," Miss Lillian told all of us. "Try to relate the question to something you know." She stopped in front of me. "Vanessa, let's have you give it a go. Tell me your thoughts on clothing that incites violence. Like the Zoot Suit Riots."

I stared at her, wide-eyed. I knew what a zoot suit was. They were oversize suits with baggy coats and wide-legged pants. My great-grandpa had worn one in the forties, and my grandma even had a photo of her sitting on his knee while he was wearing one. To me, the zoot suit looked ridiculous, but I didn't know why it'd have anything to do with riots.

"Um . . . sometimes fashion is so terrible, people fight to get rid of it?" I guessed. "But people should know that everything eventually goes out of style." I cocked my head to one side. "Did I get it right?"

Miss Lillian's pitying smile said it all. "The riots were long before you were born, so I wouldn't expect you to know. But it was a good effort! Just remember, confidence. There was a great deal of uncertainty in your voice."

"I was a great deal uncertain," I said.

"Let me see if I can do it," said Brooke, leaning forward. "Ask me a question, Miss Lillian."

Miss Lillian stroked her chin and finally asked, "How can I lower my cholesterol?"

Brooke folded her hands on her lap and glanced up at Miss Lillian. "High cholesterol can definitely be a danger, and it's good for you to be concerned. You should really consult your family doctor if you're not seeing desired results."

"Bravo!" Miss Lillian clapped the tips of her fingers together.

Brooke leaned toward me. "I got that last part from a dandruff commercial."

I snickered quietly since Miss Lillian was now talking to Heather.

"What advice would you give two people who are going through a divorce and fighting over the toaster?"

Heather took a sip of hot chocolate and then said, "The important thing in ending any relationship is keeping your dignity and humanity. If the other person wants a toaster that badly, let them have it. You can always buy another. If you lose yourself, you can't buy that back."

Brooke and I looked at each other and then at Heather.

"All hail the queen of advice," said Brooke, raising her hands high and bowing at the waist.

"Truly, we are not worthy." I covered my eyes and turned my head away.

Miss Lillian smiled. "Heather, my dear, I

believe you've earned another muffin."

After Miss Lillian returned with more muffins and hot chocolate, she drilled us with a few more questions and then had us stand side by side in front of her bathroom mirror.

"I want you to see what confidence looks like," she said. "This"—she gestured to our reflections—"isn't it."

"It's hard to be confident when you're not sure if you drank too much hot cocoa," said Brooke, fidgeting.

"This will only take a minute," Miss Lillian assured her. "Girls, heads are high, backs are arched, shoulders are strong." She moved among us, adjusting our postures. "Now look at yourselves in the mirror."

We did as she said. I had to admit, I looked pretty confident.

"Vanessa"—Miss Lillian put a hand on my back—"I understand you get stage fright."

My confident reflection faltered a little. "Yes, ma'am."

"What I want you to do when you get onstage is imagine you're talking to your reflection, not the audience. Does that make sense?"

I nodded.

"And recall a happy memory. One that makes you smile just thinking about it." She gestured to Heather and Brooke. "I want you all to try that, in fact. As Peter Pan would say, 'Think lovely, wonderful thoughts.'"

I thought for a moment and smiled at my friends in the mirror. "Hey. You guys remember in elementary school, when Heather brought a candy bar to feed the llama at the petting zoo?"

Heather's mouth dropped open, and she poked me in the side. "Don't you dare bring that up!" she said, but she was smiling.

"Yeah," Brooke said with a grin. "Except the candy bar had so much caramel that the llama couldn't stop chewing, and its teeth got stuck together."

"Perfect!" said Miss Lillian. "Now that we're all smiles—"

"But the llama's lips were still moving," I said, giggling. "And it looked like it was talking."

Heather giggled too. "And Brooke started speaking for it."

"Hi, I'm Mr. Llama," said Brooke in a deep voice. "Do you have a spare toothbrush?"

All three of us cracked up.

"Lovely anecdote," Miss Lillian said above our laughter. "And now let's dial it back a bit so we're simply smiling."

The giggles died down, and we all smiled at ourselves in the mirror.

Except when someone tells you *not* to laugh, it makes you want to laugh even harder.

"Pffft." Brooke pressed her lips together and tried to keep a straight face. Next to her,

Heather's mouth twitched, and she cleared her throat. I couldn't look at either of them.

"Now take a—"

"HA!" Brooke let out an explosive laugh and quickly clamped a hand over her mouth, but it was too late. Heather started giggling, which made me snort. Brooke began laughing behind her hand, little puffs of air coming from her nose like a steam engine. And then a booger came out of her nose, and all three of us completely lost it.

Miss Lillian sighed, and smiled. "Class dismissed."

On Friday at lunch, when we related the story to Tim, we laughed even harder, especially when Brooke reenacted the experience with a raisin coming out of her nose.

Tim chuckled and then said, "Miss Lillian can instruct you all she wants, but you really need to see good speakers in action. I have a DVD of famous political debates. Why don't we all get together tomorrow night and watch them?"

And just like that, the laughter died forever.

"But tomorrow night is Musketeer Movies," Heather reminded him.

For years, Brooke, Heather, and I, the Three Musketeers, have gotten together on Saturday nights to watch movies and have pizza at Heather's house. This year, Tim joined us, once, but it's kind of our special thing.

"The DVD is kind of like a movie," he said. "You'll enjoy it, I promise."

"But . . ." I turned to Brooke, who always had the right, but rude, words.

To my surprise, though, Brooke shrugged. "It's only one night, and we really need to do well next week." She perked up. "To make it worth it, I'll bring stuff for ice-cream sundaes, so we can reward ourselves afterward!"

"Ooh!" said Heather and I.

"Sold," I added. "I'm in."

"Me too," said Heather.

"Great!" said Tim. "Tomorrow night it is."

Katie walked up holding her lunch tray. "If it isn't the fabulous foursome! Can I join you?"

"Sure!" said Heather, scooting her tray down.

"Good, because I need to talk to Vanny, like, ASAP." She pointed her spork at me. "You need to choose your Breakfast Buddy, so we can tell the winners before the weekend."

"My what?" I asked. "I eat breakfast at home."

"Not next Monday you don't." She shook her head. "Breakfast Buddies was the last of our promotional contests, remember?"

"No! I mean . . . I saw the name for it on the flyer you made, but . . ."

Brooke spoke up. "Supposedly, you and Katie are having breakfast on Monday with two lucky students who entered ideas for teen clothing labels."

"How do you know that?" I asked.

"How else?" She shrugged. "Locker 411."

"And who are the two lucky students?" I asked, turning to Katie.

"That's what we have to decide!" She chomped on a pickle spear. "There were a lot of good entries."

"Um . . . fine." I nodded. "What do you have?"

"We'll leave you guys to work," said Heather, nodding to Brooke and Tim. The three of them picked up their lunches and moved to a different table, prompting Katie to switch her seat to one right next to mine.

"This is so exciting, don't you think?" she gushed, pulling a pagelong list out of her pocket. "By the way, what do you think of the Toastmasters videos I sent you?"

"Oh! Um . . . they're great," I said. "I'm really learning a lot."

In actuality, I hadn't even opened the email

from Katie, with the subject line "Toasty!"

Instead of enjoying a relaxing lunch with my friends, I was forced to pore over names of nonexistent clothing labels with Katie, in preparation for a breakfast I didn't even want to have. We finally settled on Top of the Morning, for a brand of T-shirts, and Buy the Seat of Our Pants, for a brand of jeans. Katie wolfed down the rest of her lunch and pranced off to tell the winners and post the information in Locker 411.

Then instead of having loads of laughs in Journalism while we worked on the advice column, the "Lincoln's Letters" team sat through a lecture from Mary Patrick on how she expected us to behave during the advice-offs.

But all of that was still better than the debate DVD Tim showed us Saturday night. We were only five minutes into the first debate when the audience started booing one of the candidates.

"Oh no," I said, clutching a pillow to myself.

"What if that happens to us? What if people boo after our answers?"

"It's not going to happen," Heather assured me.

"Not where we can hear it, anyway," added Tim. Brooke elbowed him. "What? It's true! We'll be filming in the auditorium, and all the students will be in classrooms."

"That's not why I elbowed you!" said Brooke.

Meanwhile, things on the debate DVD started getting pretty intense, and soon, the candidates were adding insults about the other candidates in their answers.

I looked over to Heather, who shook her head. "It's not going to happen. Katie adores you."

"But she has no filter," I said. "She might insult me without even realizing it."

"Guys, you're not paying attention to the speakers!" said Tim. "Watch their movements and their facial expressions."

"I already know how to wave my fist angrily

and frown," said Brooke. "I should run for mayor."

Tim sighed. "Listen to their voices. The power."

The two candidates quickly got into a shouting match, each trying to talk louder than the other.

"Sounds like my brothers fighting over the remote," mused Heather.

"You're not even trying," said Tim. He got up and then headed for the kitchen.

"Don't go, it's just getting good!" Brooke shouted after him. "One of them is using big words I don't know!"

I shushed her and found Tim banging an ice cube tray on the counter. "Hey, don't be mad," I said. "They're just trying to make me feel better."

"I'm not mad," said Tim with a smile. "I'm thirsty." He plopped some ice into a glass and put the tray back into the freezer.

"So you're just wandering around Heather's house?" I asked.

"She told me to make myself at home when I came in," he said. "This is what I'd do at home." He poured soda into the glass. "You know, you shouldn't freak out about the advice-off. It's not a big deal, and it's definitely not as embarrassing as prancing around in tights and a skirt." At my quizzical expression, he added, "Recurring nightmare of mine."

"You can say it's not a big deal because you don't freeze up," I said. "I do."

"I know," he said. "And last time it happened, we took the attention off you as fast as we could. Which is what we'd do if it happened again. We're not going to let you suffer, V."

He had a point. I knew my teammates would never abandon me. But it felt better to have one of them say it.

"Thanks," I told him.

Heather appeared in the doorway. "Everything okay? Brooke's not having as much fun insulting Tim's DVD without him."

"Lucky me," he said, picking up his glass. Before we headed back into the living room, he turned to me. "Remember, it's no big deal."

And I believed him for the rest of the weekend. Then Monday morning came.

One thing I had to give Katie credit for was the amazing breakfast she'd put together for the two of us and the contest winners. There were blueberry muffins, fruit salad, orange juice, crispy bacon, and potatoes with bell peppers.

"Just a little something my mom threw together," she said when the contest winners and I oohed and aahed.

"Katie, this is amazing," I said.

"If it's worth doing, it's worth doing right!" she told me with a wink. "Besides, we're kind of a big deal. It'd look cheap if we served granola bars and juice boxes."

"Well, it's not that big a deal," I said, repeating Tim's words.

"Sure it is!" said one of the contest winners. "You guys are the talk of the school."

"We should be the talk of the *town!*" said Katie.

"Should we, though?" I asked, snapping a piece of bacon in half. "It's really not that big a deal. I mean . . . an advice-off for a middle-school newspaper?" I scoffed.

My Breakfast Buddies stopped eating. Katie smiled at the two winners.

"Would you excuse us for just a sec? And help yourself to some more potatoes. They're gluten free!" She grabbed my arm and pulled me several yards away. "Vanny, I love you to pieces, and you know I think that every word from your mouth is glitter and diamonds—"

"Glitter and diamonds?" I repeated.

"But you have to stop downplaying this whole thing," Katie finished. "It is absolutely a big deal, and we want it to be a bigger deal."

"I don't!" I said.

"Yes, you do," said Katie. "Don't you get it? If we make this into a big enough deal, it not only makes the school paper, it makes the local paper! It may even get us on TV!"

"It may?" My stomach gurgled at the thought.

"Yes! And at the very least, we owe it to these girls to make them feel like something special," she said, tugging my arm. "So let's have a happy, big-deal breakfast."

We sat back down, and I smiled and pushed food around on my plate, but I didn't feel like a big deal at all.

CHAPTER 7

Brooke and the Boys

When the bell rang for the start of school, kids scattered for their homerooms, but I made my way toward the auditorium. The entire news team had been invited to watch the advice-off from where it was being broadcast, and there was no way I'd miss a chance to cheer on my friends.

"Hey, V!" Heather called to me from the sixth-grade hall. I paused so she could catch up, and she broke into a run.

"Oh, you don't have to hurry!" I told her.

"It's good exercise for choir," she said. "We

have to be able to move and sing at the same time."

I crossed my arms. "How come I didn't get a song?"

She smiled and bumped my shoulder. "How was Breakfast Buddies?"

"Delicious and daunting," I said. "According to Katie, this is a really big deal."

Heather made a face. "That probably doesn't help your stage fright."

"Not even a little," I said. "Uh-oh. What's going on here?"

Mary Patrick was pacing the doorway leading to the auditorium. As soon as she saw me and Heather, she stormed over.

"Have you seen Tim? He's late."

"He's Tim," I reminded her. "But don't worry, he'll be here. He wouldn't miss the chance to appear in front of hundreds of girls."

Mary Patrick's face was as blank as a

mannequin's. "We only have twenty minutes to do this."

"It'll be fine," I reassured her. "Tim will get here, and until he does, go with Brooke."

Mary Patrick frowned but nodded. "Fine. We'll start without him."

We followed her into the auditorium, where several people were already milling about. Brooke was talking to Tim's competition, a guy named Luke, while her competition, Ryan, was flipping through *Sports Illustrated*.

Gil was the only one actually sitting in the audience, shouting things to Stefan, who fiddled with a video camera on a tripod at the front of the stage. A thick length of cables ran from the camera to somewhere offstage to link with the school's video feed.

There were two chairs positioned farther back onstage, bright lights shining on them. Soon, hundreds of eyes would be on those two chairs. And tomorrow I'd be in one of them.

"Hey." Heather tapped my arm, and I yelped, throwing my hands into the air.

Everyone turned to see what was happening.

"We're . . . uh . . . practicing a new dance move for my party!" said Heather. She yelped and threw her hands into the air.

Worst. Save. Ever. But I gave her a grateful smile when people went back to what they were doing.

"You okay?" she asked.

"Not if we really have to do that at your party," I said. When she didn't laugh, I nodded. "I'm fine. Just nervous about tomorrow."

"Aww." She rubbed my arm. "Those Toastmasters videos Katie gave you didn't help?"

"Oh, they're great," I said, giving her a thumbs-up. I'd finally opened the files over the weekend. "I can now confidently say . . . *bonjour*."

Heather wrinkled her forehead. "Huh?"

"She accidentally gave me videos on how to speak French," I said.

"Seriously?"

"*Oui.*"

Stefan crouched on the edge of the stage and whistled to us. "Hey, can one of you come up here? I need some help, and you two are the most photogenic."

"Sure!" said Heather, blushing. She took the hand he offered and climbed onstage.

I went and sat in the audience next to Gil, who was now attaching a lens to his camera.

"Wait, we're filming this *and* taking photos?" I asked. Just what I needed . . . photographic evidence of me fainting onstage.

"Stefan wanted me to capture shots of him capturing footage of the advice-off," Gil said, adjusting the focus.

I wasn't surprised. Stefan was the kind of guy who'd wink at his own reflection.

"He doesn't see his name enough under every photo in the paper?" I asked.

Gil shrugged. "I don't mind. It's a chance for me to get a photo credit," he said with a goofy grin. "I'm just lucky Stefan didn't rig an automatic timer so he could take photos of himself."

"Oh, I'm sure it's coming," I said with a laugh.

Gil raised the camera and aimed it at me. "Perfect shot!"

The flash went off, and I was blinking away pretty little stars.

"Oh! Gil—"

"Sorry," he said. "I have to test the lighting." He turned the camera around so I could see the preview screen. "What do you think?"

I leaned over and braced myself for whatever widemouthed moment he'd managed to capture, but somehow he'd managed to get me midsmile.

"Hey, not bad!" I said, reaching for the camera. "Can I get a better peek?"

"Sure, but be careful," he said. "This is a two-thousand-dollar camera."

I pulled back my empty hands. "Never mind."

Gil smiled and lifted the camera closer for my inspection.

In the photo, my eyes were shining, my cheekbones were killer, and my dimples brought out my smile even more.

"This is way better than the one Stefan took. How did you make me so pretty?" I asked.

"I didn't make you pretty; you are pretty." Gil grinned and blushed. "Don't let that go to your head."

"Too late. Already on permanent replay," I said. "If you say it again, I could even make it my ringtone."

Gil laughed. "All joking aside, the photographer doesn't make something happen that isn't already there. We just know what to look for and how to draw it out. Like you do when you offer beauty tips."

I grinned. "I like that."

It was a good thing I wasn't holding the two-thousand-dollar camera because a second later, Mary Patrick shouted by my ear, "Finally!"

I turned to see what she was looking at. Tim was running into the auditorium, his book bag dragging on the ground behind him.

"Sorry I'm late!" he called breathlessly. "I was—"

"Taking your books for a walk?" asked Brooke.

He gave her a withering look. "The strap broke."

"Save your sob story," said Mary Patrick. "We have a show to put on." She clapped her hands and shouted, "Places, people!"

Nobody moved.

"When you say places . . ."

"Oh, for Pete's sake." Mary Patrick smacked

a hand to her forehead. "Brooke and Ryan in the chairs onstage, Stefan behind the video camera, Gil on the side with the regular camera, and everyone else sitting down and being quiet!" Her hands flew in every direction as she spoke, like a deranged flight attendant.

Brooke took a running leap and bounded up onto the stage without using her hands. Not to be outdone, Ryan tried to copy her. There was a ripping sound when he went airborne and a double *THUNK!* as he hit the stage with his knees. He gave a slight whimper but tried to play it off with a combination swagger-hobble.

"Smooth," said Brooke. "Are you going to stumble on your answers as much as you stumbled onstage?"

"You just watch," he said with a scowl. "Then when the entire school picks me, go home and play with Barbie dolls while I write the sports advice."

She rolled her eyes as they took their seats,

then turned to Mary Patrick. "Can we end this foolishness already?"

Mary Patrick regarded both of them with a stern gaze. "This will be a live feed. Brooke, I trust you to not screw it up." She fixed her eyes on Ryan until he shifted uncomfortably in his seat. "But, Ryan, if you even utter the first letter of a curse word, you will rue the day you ever crossed paths with Mary Patrick Stephens. Understand?"

Ryan swallowed hard and nodded. Brooke leaned toward him.

"When *she* plays with Barbie dolls, she snaps their heads off," Brooke told him.

Mary Patrick whirled around to face everyone else. "The rest of you . . . absolute silence. Stefan, count down from five, and let's go."

He nodded. "Five, four, three, two, one." Then he pointed to Mary Patrick.

"Good morning, fellow—"

"ACHOO!" I sneezed, drowning her out.

Her head snapped down as she gave me a death stare, but she continued talking.

"Good morning, fellow students, and welcome to this live broadcast of the *Lincoln Log*'s advice-off. You will be the ones to decide who gives better advice: our esteemed columnists or the most average among you." She pointed to Brooke and Ryan, respectively. Brooke smiled at the camera while Ryan picked at one of his teeth with a finger.

"I'll be presenting five questions to each set of contestants," said Mary Patrick. "They'll have one minute to write short answers on their dry-erase boards and one minute to present them to you. If you like an answer, you choose that contestant. Our first two contestants are Brooke Jacobs and Ryan Durstwich. I'll be asking them questions in the areas of sports and fitness. Contestants, are you ready?"

Brooke and Ryan both nodded, holding their dry-erase boards in their laps.

"Question one: I'm a bit overweight but want to get into sports. What can you recommend for me?"

Ryan smirked and instantly bowed his head to start writing. Brooke stared thoughtfully into space and then started writing as well.

With nothing to say for the next minute, Mary Patrick just stared into the camera with a tight smile, occasionally checking her stopwatch.

At the end of the minute, she commanded Brooke and Ryan to show her their boards.

"What sports can you recommend?" she asked.

Ryan flipped his board first. "Any sport that allows you to throw your weight around, like football or wrestling." He made a fist. "Use it to crush your opponent!"

"Football and wrestling are fine," said Brooke. "But what about for overweight girls?"

Ryan wrinkled his nose. "Um . . ."

I wasn't a fortune-teller, but something told me he'd lose a large portion of the female vote with that.

Brooke flipped her sign next. "Golf," she said. "It doesn't rely on extreme aerobic activity like other sports, and it allows you to lose weight while you walk from hole to hole."

Score one for Brooke.

Mary Patrick's next question, "How can I be in the Olympics?," was met with a laugh from Ryan and the answer, "Are you serious? Make a really big wish on your next birthday." Brooke, meanwhile, said, "Get a coach, train, practice, and qualify. Good luck!"

With just those two questions, I knew she already had it in the bag. At the end of their round, Brooke offered to shake Ryan's hand, but he smirked and jumped off the stage, a gaping hole visible in the back of his pants.

Tim and Luke were up next, and I had to admit, Luke seemed to know his stuff. But Tim was funnier and more charming.

"Why do guys always text back one-word answers?" asked Mary Patrick.

We're busy and not big texters to begin with, Luke wrote on his board.

We're busy, but we want to say something so you know we still like you was Tim's answer, along with a wink.

Heather, Brooke, and I looked at one another and laughed quietly. In every classroom, at least one girl with *Mrs. Tim Antonides* on her notebook was no doubt sighing happily.

The final question was a tricky one.

"I'm a guy who likes two different girls, and they both like me. The problem is that they're best friends. How do I choose between them?" asked Mary Patrick.

Both Luke and Tim made faces before writing on their dry-erase boards.

"Find someone new to like," said Luke. "You don't want to get in the middle of that mess."

"Clone yourself," said Tim. "That's the only way you'll make it out alive."

Mary Patrick smiled at their answers and spoke to the camera. "That concludes today's advice-off. Don't forget to fill out your ballots, and tune in tomorrow for relationships and fashion tips." She nodded to Stefan, who stopped the recording, and we all clapped, including Mary Patrick.

"Good job, everyone. I'll see you later in Journalism. Vanessa?" She gingerly climbed off the stage and stood in front of me.

I regarded her with wide eyes. Mary Patrick had spoken to me by name. That *never* happened.

In the newsroom, I think she just sees a pile of fashionable clothing sitting on a chair.

"That's me," I said, just to keep the record straight.

"I've been checking out all the promo stuff you put together for your advice-off."

I took a deep breath. "I can explain—"

"It's good stuff," said Mary Patrick. "And you've increased awareness for the entire paper. Way to go."

I blushed, both for her kind words and because I didn't deserve credit for them. "Thanks, but—"

"Just make sure you can deliver tomorrow," she said, stepping closer to me. In a quiet, dangerous voice, she added, "You promised the students the showdown of the century, and you better give them one."

She clapped me on the shoulder, almost

knocking me down, and hurried off to speak to Stefan.

Katie promised the showdown!, I wanted to shout after her. Instead, I grabbed my book bag and wondered if anyone with the flu would be willing to sneeze on me.

CHAPTER

8

Katie, Katie Everywhere

I'd kind of been hoping the advice-off would be a flop, that kids would see it and say to themselves, *Lame! I'll definitely skip tomorrow, especially the fashion segment.*

But because fashion is awesome, I knew that would never happen, and because nowadays everyone is crazy about reality TV, the advice-off had even the lunch lady talking.

"Can you believe that one Ryan boy? Laughing at someone's Olympic dreams." She shook her head as she dropped a handful of tater tots on my plate.

"Yeah," I said in a vague voice. "Can I have some salad, too, please?"

"Oh, but the other fellow, Tim what's his name . . . Antenna? My niece would love him."

"Mm-hmm," I said, handing her my meal card.

She swiped it, but instead of giving it back, she pointed it at me. "You look familiar."

"Yeah, I was in a baby food ad when I was one," I told her, plucking the card from her fingers. "Thanks!"

To be fair, I really was in a baby food ad, and my mom got free jars of Delicious Squish for a year. But I knew the lunch lady was thinking of the advice-off flyers, and I didn't want to hear her gush about how wonderful Katie was.

I joined my friends at our lunch table, putting my tray down next to Tim's.

"The lunch lady found you a girlfriend," I informed him.

He spat a mouthful of soda across the table. That made me feel a little better.

"Dude!" cried Brooke, wiping off her math book. "And you could do a lot worse than the lunch lady. Imagine all the free corn dogs you'll get."

"No, no, the lunch lady doesn't want to date him," I said. "She wants her *niece* to date him."

"Okay, so no free corn dogs, but you'll probably get a twenty-percent family discount, which at a dollar fifty apiece would be"—Brooke scrunched her face—"thirty cents off?"

I nodded, and Brooke triumphantly slammed her book shut.

"I am going to ace this quiz. Math. Genius." She pointed to herself.

"Hey, math genius," said Heather, sitting beside her. "You guys did great today!"

"Thanks!" Brooke grinned. "That was

actually a lot of fun, even if my competition was an obnoxious pig."

"You'll definitely win that one," said Tim. "Although, someone else might be writing my column next week." He made a face.

Brooke leaned back and crossed her arms. "Well, well. This is quite a change."

"What do you mean?" asked Tim.

"I seem to recall someone didn't want to write for the advice column a month ago, and now you're sweatin' it that someone's going to take your job."

"Oooh!" said Heather and I.

Tim scoffed. "Please. I'm not sweatin' it. Check 'em."

He raised his arms so we could inspect the pits.

"Lovely," I said. "But some of us are still eating." I lowered the arm closest to me.

"And even if he beats me," Tim continued, "he only gets the job for a week, which frees me up to do more sports coverage while Stefan shoots people."

All three of us gave him horrified looks.

"With his camera!" Tim quickly added. "Shoots people with his camera. Apparently, there's this big exhibit on Friday that he's trying to get into."

"Really? I wonder if Gil knows about that," I said.

Tim shrugged. "Anyway, if I lose, I still get plenty of paper time. It's win-win."

"Win-win-winners!" chirped Katie, appearing out of nowhere, like a pimple on date night.

She plopped down on my lap, stealing a tater tot.

"Oh, these need way more salt." She grabbed a shaker and unleashed a blizzard on my tray. "Hi, you guys!"

"Hi, Katie!" Heather said.

"Hey, Katie!" Brooke said.

"Hey there," Tim said.

"That's too much salt," I said.

But nobody heard me.

Brooke slapped a hand on the table. "Katie, I never found the balloon with the ribbon in it! Do you realize what I went through? How many people I had to push down?"

"Brooke!" Heather gave her a shocked look, and Brooke blushed.

"It was only one person."

"Not better," said Heather.

Katie laughed and grabbed Brooke's hands. "If it means that much to you, I have another pair of tickets with your name all over them."

Brooke squealed and leaned across the table to hug Katie, dragging her over my salad.

"Hey, leave my lunch out of this!" I poked Katie in the side, and she jumped up, laughing.

"Sorry, Vanny." She brushed a piece of lettuce off the front of her sweater. "I actually came by to tell you that I was talking to James . . . uh . . . Principal Winslow," she corrected herself, "and he said they've already received a ton of ballots in the office from today's advice-off."

Tim perked up. "Am I winning?"

Katie shrugged. "He wouldn't give me the details, but from what other kids are telling me, you're going to win."

Tim smirked and crossed his arms behind his head. "Ha! I mean . . . not that I was sweatin' it or anything."

"We know," I said, lowering the arm closest to me again. "You already showed us your armpits."

Tim laughed nervously and avoided Katie's eye. "Whaaat? That was stretching."

But Katie was too busy looking at her watch. "OMG, I've gotta go! I promised I'd do a guest lecture in Home Economics."

"Lecture?" I repeated. "On what?"

"Fashion, of course!" Katie tweaked my nose with her fingers. I kind of wanted to tweak hers with my fist.

"Wow!" said Heather. "That's really amazing. You're like a kid genius."

"Oh, stop!" Katie giggled. "I'm just talking about what I know."

Brooke raised an eyebrow. "V, I think you're going to have some fierce competition tomorrow."

"That's right! You better bring your A game, sister," said Katie, touching me for the hundredth time. "Well, I'd love to keep basking in the gorgeous glow coming from this table, but I must be off to spread wisdom. *Au revoir!*"

"Huh?" Brooke said as Katie pranced away.

"It means 'good-bye' in French," I said.

"How do you know that?"

"It's a long story," I said. Out of the corner of my eye, I saw Heather smile.

In Journalism, the topic on everyone's mind? The advice-off. After Mrs. H addressed issues with the issue, we talked about the morning's event. People congratulated Brooke and Tim, weighing the odds of each win (nobody thought either of them would lose). Then the attention turned to me and Heather. Before anyone could start placing bets, I raised my hand.

"Could we please talk about something other than the advice-off? We still have a paper to put out, don't we?"

Mrs. H smiled. "Vanessa does have a point. Let's get some ideas going for our next issue. Mary Patrick?"

Mary Patrick nodded and uncapped her marker with a loud pop, pen poised at the board.

"Front page?" she called over her shoulder. "What are you working on for this week?"

A guy leaning against a cabinet said, "Front page is covering the advice-offs."

And we were back on that ride.

"We should have the write-ups done by Thursday morning, after Heather and Vanessa have competed and the results for both advice-offs are in," he continued.

Mrs. H gave him a thumbs-up. "And where are we with photos for the front page?"

Gil glanced up from where he was drawing on one of his sneakers. "I have the proofs from today right here." He leaned over and patted his backpack.

"Well, let's see them," said Stefan, extending a hand. "How do they look?"

I knew he really meant *How do I look?*

Stefan opened the envelope and flipped through the photos. From where I sat, they looked fine, but Stefan said, "What lens did you use? They're so far away. You can barely see my . . . their faces."

Gil shrugged. "I was trying to capture the

whole scene, not just one person," he said pointedly.

Mrs. H leaned over Stefan's shoulder. "I think these pictures are fine, Gil. Although a few close-ups wouldn't hurt tomorrow."

Gil nodded and went back to drawing on his shoe.

"What else is on the front page?" asked Mary Patrick.

"The tour of the Ecklesby Estate," said an eighth-grade girl. "It's one of the oldest houses in the city, and it's about to be torn down, so the eighth graders are going there tomorrow on a field trip."

Mrs. H nodded. "Fascinating! Let's make sure we get some good photos, Stefan."

He snorted. "Of an old house? You got it."

Mary Patrick scribbled on the board. "Sports?"

"I'm doing a piece on the fund raiser to replace the football team's helmets," said Stefan.

"And I'm covering the new mascot," said Tim.

Mrs. H and Mary Patrick continued through the pages of the paper, and then we broke into our small groups. Brooke had already grabbed the advice requests from the box and spread them on the table for us to choose.

"Hmmm," said Tim. "The hilarious part of me wants to answer the guy who challenged me to a rap battle. . . ."

Heather, Brooke, and I laughed.

"While the newly compassionate me wants to help this girl pick a present for her boyfriend," he finished.

"Rap battle!" cried Brooke, looking to me and Heather. "Rap battle!"

We took up the chant. "Rap battle! Rap battle!"

Tim grinned. "I thought you wanted me to

care more about other people's problems."

"You can answer her question on the website," Brooke reminded him.

"Rap battle! Rap battle!" Heather and I kept chanting.

"Fair enough. Mix Master Tim in the house!" he said, striking a pose.

"Okay," said Brooke, chuckling. "Now help me find one."

The four of us went back to sorting through the requests.

"Wow," I said as the piles in front of Brooke and Tim grew. "A lot of these are about fitness or asking for guy advice."

"It's not surprising," said a voice from behind us. Mary Patrick strolled by. "It's called increased awareness. Students saw Brooke and Tim this morning, and now their interest is piqued." She nodded to me and Heather. "I expect the two of you will have your share of extra questions after tomorrow's advice-off."

Heather's eyes shone. "Oh, I hope so! Imagine all the people we could help!"

Ever the kind heart.

Tim lifted his pile of questions and let them flutter onto the table. "Imagine if these were hundred-dollar bills. We should really charge for our answers."

Ever the schemer.

Brooke snorted. "If the advice of four twelve-year-olds was that valuable, I'm pretty sure we'd be so famous, we wouldn't go to regular school."

Ever the realist.

"Give me a few years," I told my friends. "When my designs make it out into the world, I will be charging for my time."

Ever the dreamer.

When school ended for the day, I rushed to the auditorium but lingered at the entrance, poking my head inside. The place was empty, and the drama club wouldn't show up for at least ten minutes.

I had the place all to myself.

Dropping my bags in the front row, I climbed onto the stage.

"Hello," I said to the empty chairs. My back was hunched, as if I was ready to curl into a ball at the first sign of predators. I straightened and then put my hands on my hips. "Hey!" I tried in a cheerier voice. "Hi! I'm Vanessa—"

The side door opened, and I quickly leaped down, landing on all fours.

"Vanny?" Katie tilted her head to one side.

"Katie?" I sat back on my heels. "What are you doing here?"

"I'm helping with costumes," she said, holding up a sewing box.

"What?" There wasn't an ounce of happiness

in my voice, but Katie smiled all the same.

"Isn't this great? We get to make the costumes together!"

"But I've already started," I said. "And there isn't enough work for two people."

Katie settled on the carpet beside me. "Don't be silly! There are two costume changes, and five actors. You're really going to sew ten costumes by yourself? No, no, no. I have come to save the day." She made muscles with both her arms. "Now what are you doing on the floor?"

"Uh . . . yoga," I said. "I really like the peace and quiet of being alone."

I could not have emphasized the word *alone* stronger, except maybe with a bullhorn. But Katie smiled again and snapped her fingers.

"You were doing Cat-Cow? I'll join you!" She got on her hands and knees.

"Oh! Uh . . ." I imitated her.

"Are you on Cat or Cow?" she asked.

"Well . . ." I didn't know any yoga except the breathing Heather had shown me, but cats seemed more glamorous than cows. "Cat."

Katie bowed her head and curved her spine upward like a hissing cat. I copied her.

"How long do you hold your poses?" she asked.

"Until I feel ridiculous, which is now," I said.

Katie raised her head and dropped her spine so that her back curved into a U. I guessed this was the cow.

The auditorium door opened again, and several people walked in. I started to get up, but Katie grabbed my arm. "Let's have them join us!" she said.

"What?" Again, no joy. I wasn't sure how Katie maintained such a constant state of obliviousness.

"Guys! Vanessa is leading us in yoga!" she called.

"No! I—"

"Yoga? Great idea!" said Phoebe. "We need to loosen up our muscles. Everyone onstage!"

The actors and actresses, along with Katie, put away their schoolbags and did as Phoebe instructed.

"Come on, Vanny!" Katie offered me a hand up.

"Oh, I think I should stay down here where you can . . . um . . . all see me better." I laughed nervously as everyone faced me.

After several seconds of awkward staring, I realized they were waiting for me to start.

"So . . . uh . . . our first pose is . . ." I didn't actually name it, but I stretched my right hand high into the sky and wiggled my fingers.

Everyone mirrored me except one girl who frowned. "I'm not familiar with this pose. Is it a modified version of the Gate pose?"

Why wasn't this girl in charge?

"Uh . . . no. This is a different type of yoga from my . . . my ancestors." I clasped my hands together solemnly. "That first pose is actually called . . . Teacher, Teacher." I lifted my left arm and wiggled my fingers. "And now we do it on the other side."

Everyone shifted along with me. Yoga was supposed to be relaxing, but I was racking my brain, trying to come up with the next move.

"Uh . . . this one is Back Scratch." I lifted my right hand up to scratch my left shoulder blade. It actually felt pretty good.

After Back Scratch, I showed them Who's Following Me?, I Dropped My Keys, Sumo Wrestler . . .

"And these are from your *ancestors*?" asked Yoga Girl at one point.

I put my finger to my lips and shifted into the

next pose, Rock in My Shoe. I had to fight back a smile at how dumb they all looked doing my made-up yoga. It only made me more confident that I had no desire to be in the spotlight.

CHAPTER

9

Heather the Parrot

"**W**hat do you mean you're not going onstage?" Brooke demanded the next morning.

I'd asked her, Heather, and Tim to meet me around the corner from school so I could tell them my plan.

"Katie has built this up to be too big of a deal, and I already have massive stage fright," I said. "If I get up on that stage, I'm going to lose. The only way I can win is with a little help from Heather."

"Me?" Heather squeaked. "I don't know anything about fashion."

"I know," I said. "Your shoes never match your purse. But that's okay!" I stopped her before she could interject. "You're just going to repeat what I tell you."

I reached into my backpack and pulled out a set of wireless earbuds with an attached mic. "Here. You can talk and hear me through these. They'll hardly be visible on camera, so it'll look more professional."

Heather gave me a dubious look but synched the earbuds with her phone and put them in.

"Uh . . . hello?" Tim waved a hand. "Why don't we just tell Mary Patrick and ask—"

"No!" I shook my head vehemently. "If we tell her, she'll freak out and force me onstage. Then I'll freak out. Just . . . Heather, when you're done with your questions and it's my turn, stay in the seat."

Heather blinked at me. "I'm pretty sure she can tell us apart."

"Duh." I rolled my eyes. "Again, you're not pretending to be me. You're just speaking for me. And Mary Patrick won't want to make a scene in front of the whole school, so she'll have to go along with it."

"And then later kill you behind the cafeteria Dumpster," Brooke told me.

"That's why I have these." I held out a jumbo bag of Reese's mini-cups, Mary Patrick's greatest weakness.

"I don't know," said Tim. "You're going to have to throw that bag pretty hard to knock her out."

I gave him a withering look. "Do not make me practice on you."

Tim held up his hands and backed away. Brooke stepped between us.

"V, are you sure you want to do this? It has BAD IDEA written all over it in blue and green, and I know you hate when colors clash."

I gripped her shoulders. "Trust me. It's this

or we're all mopping up my puke during home-room."

Brooke clapped her hands. "Okay! Let's test out the earbuds. Vanessa, give Heather a call."

I pulled my phone out of my pocket and dialed Heather's number.

"Hello?" she said.

"Can you hear me?" I said.

She turned to me. "Yes, but to be fair, you're standing right next to me."

I walked around the corner and whispered, "Can you hear me?"

Heather whispered back, "Yes."

I hung up and joined the others.

"Okay, call me when it's my turn. After Mary Patrick reads the question, repeat it back to me and wait for my answer," I told her.

"Where are you going to be?" asked Brooke.

"I'll be in the nurse's office," I said. "On Tues-days, she gets in after homeroom, so I can hide in there during the advice-off."

Tim studied me. "You know the nurse's schedule? How often do you see her?"

I cleared my throat. "She's thinking of naming the waiting room after me."

The bell rang, and all four of us headed into the building.

"What are you going to say is wrong with you?" asked Brooke.

"I'll just go with something vague. Dizziness and blurred vision," I said.

Then I tripped over my own foot and fell.

"Well, nobody would ever doubt you," said Tim as he and Brooke helped me up.

Heather started to brush the gravel away, but I stopped her.

"Leave it there for added effect," I said.

Then I hobbled toward the main office. A woman I'd never seen before was volunteering at the front desk. Perfect!

"Can I help you?" she asked.

"I need to see the nurse," I said, pointing to my dirty knees. "I fell down."

She frowned. "Did you hit your head?"

"No," I said, "but I'm afraid to keep moving around in case I do."

The woman nodded and led me into the nurse's office. "Wait here. I'm sure she'll be in shortly."

I settled back on the cot and smiled at my own brilliance. All I had to do was wait for Heather's phone call. I glanced around and spotted a TV in the corner. I could even watch the advice-off from here!

Peeking into the main office to make sure nobody saw, I crept across the room and climbed onto a cabinet to turn on the TV. It blared for a second, and I fumbled to turn it down, glancing over my shoulder. Nobody came to check on the commotion.

The screen was blue, but the school's logo appeared in the bottom corner, so I knew I had the right channel. I went back to the cot and sat down to watch.

Two minutes later, the blue feed was replaced by a view of the stage. The camera focused on Mary Patrick, who wore a tight smile.

"Good morning, students. This is day two of our advice-off. Up first will be our relationship columnist, Heather Schwartz, and her opponent, Misha Danforth."

Both girls waved, and Heather even ventured a gap-toothed smile.

Mary Patrick reexplained the rules, and the girls got their dry-erase boards ready.

"The first question is: How can I tell a boy that I don't like him without hurting his feelings?"

Misha squinted thoughtfully, Heather gazed off to the side, and then they both started scribbling furiously.

After one minute, Mary Patrick called time and asked for their answers.

"The important thing is to *tell* him," said Heather, pointing to her board. "Sometimes people wait for a crush to fade, but that's just leading the other person on. If you really want to spare his feelings, you'll tell him the truth as politely as possible."

Misha turned her own board around. "Try and see things from his point of view so you can give the kindest response. Say something positive and then let him down gently."

"Oh, good answer!" said Heather.

I smacked my hand to my forehead. "Don't support the competition!" I told the TV.

Even Mary Patrick looked annoyed, but she continued to the next question. I hated to admit it, but Heather was actually in danger of losing. Her opponent had great answers, and Heather cheering her after each one only helped her more.

As they answered the final question, though, I saw a change in Heather's demeanor. She sat with her board facing her chest, legs wiggling, as if she wanted to sprint offstage as soon as she could.

"Hang in there," I whispered to the TV.

After she and Misha answered their final questions, Misha shook Heather's hand and walked offstage. But Heather continued to sit there and stare straight ahead, fingers gripping the dry-erase board until her nail beds were white.

"Heather?" Mary Patrick whispered as Katie took the now-empty seat next to Heather. "You can leave now."

Heather's eyes shifted to the camera and then to Mary Patrick.

"I will not be leaving," she said in a loud voice. "I will be speaking on behalf of Vanessa Jackson who has taken ill . . . with illness."

"What?!" Mary Patrick said at the same time as Katie.

Heather reached down and picked up her phone. "But she will still be communicating with me through this."

Mary Patrick turned an unflattering blotchy shade, and Katie pressed her lips together tightly.

"Way to not make it awkward." I sighed. Heather put in the earbuds and fidgeted with her phone. A moment later, mine rang.

"Hey, Heather," I said.

"Hey, it's Heather," she said.

"I know," I said, rolling my eyes. "I'm ready when you are."

She nodded and glanced to Mary Patrick. "We may begin!" she said loudly.

The fire in Mary Patrick's eyes looked hot enough to barbecue Heather in her chair, but just like I'd thought, she simply began speaking to the camera.

Someone knocked on the door of the nurse's office, and I practically jumped out of my skin.

"Hello?" singsonged Nurse Patti, poking her head into the room. "Is that my favorite patient I see?"

"Nurse Patti!" I gasped, tucking my phone up my right sleeve. "I thought you didn't come until late on Tuesdays."

"Most Tuesdays, dear," she said, opening a file cabinet and rifling through the folders. "But water aerobics was canceled because the instructor found out she's allergic to chlorine." She clucked her tongue. "It might take them weeks to find a replacement."

I nodded politely, feeling the weight of the phone against my wrist.

"Didn't you have something special going on this morning?" asked Nurse Patti. "I could've sworn I saw flyers. . . ."

"I got someone to fill in," I said, glancing past

Nurse Patti to the TV. To my horror, Mary Patrick was reading from a notecard.

The first question.

And I had my phone up my sleeve.

Nurse Patti pulled out my file, which was way too thick for someone who'd only been in school a month. I slowly raised the sleeve with my phone close to my ear.

"So, Miss Jackson, how are we feeling today?" she asked.

At the same time, Heather said, "What looks should I avoid this fall?"

I turned my head toward my sleeve and mumbled, "Anything pink."

"I'm sorry?" Nurse Patti closed the folder.

"What?" asked Heather.

I smiled at Nurse Patti. "Uh . . . sorry, could you repeat the question?"

Nurse Patti and Heather spoke at the same time.

"How are you feeling?"

"What's out of style?"

"Not you!" I hissed at my sleeve.

"'Not you'?" repeated Nurse Patti.

"Not shoes," I said with an airy laugh. "I am not feeling these shoes I wore." I wiggled my feet. "Bad fashion choice."

I raised my right arm to rub my shoulder.

Heather whispered, "Is that your answer? Shoes aren't in fashion?"

"Pink!" I said louder. "Pink and paisley!"

Nurse Patti froze with a thermometer in hand. "Vanessa, dear, are you okay?"

"What? Fine!" I said in my cheeriest voice. "I'm . . . pink and paisley! It's a new expression. It means everything is great."

"Huh." She shook her head. "I'll never understand what you kids come up with." She approached me with the thermometer just as Heather's answer appeared on-screen.

Pink and paisley shoes.

"Nooo!" I said.

"It's only for a minute, dear!" said Nurse Patti, wrinkling her forehead. "You've done this dozens of times!"

On TV, Heather sat up straighter and wide-eyed, looking down at her board.

"You said shoes, pink and paisley!" I saw and heard her say.

But all I could do with the thermometer in my mouth was groan. It beeped, and Nurse Patti checked the digital readout.

"Temperature's fine," she said, making a note. "What brings you in today?"

While Mary Patrick read the next question, I blurted, "My vision's a little blurry!"

"Hmm." Nurse Patti studied my chart. "Well, it's been a while since your last eye exam. And it could explain why you're so prone to bumping into things."

Mary Patrick's mouth stopped moving, and I lifted my phone sleeve by my ear.

"What are some couture designers that kids my age can afford?" asked Heather.

"Come with me so we can look at the eye chart," said Nurse Patti.

"Diffusion lines, like Miss Wu from Jason Wu, and Cut 25 from Yigal Azrouël," I said into my sleeve as I followed Nurse Patti.

She patted a stool across the room from an eye chart. "Have a seat."

I sat and took the small paddle she gave me to cover my eye.

"How do you spell the second name?" asked Heather.

"Cover your right eye and read as far down the line as you can."

I cursed under my breath and spoke into my sleeve. "*Y-I-G-A-L*—"

Nurse Patti gave me an absurd look. "You

want to try that again? Nothing you just mentioned is on here."

"Thanks for the hint," I told her with a nervous laugh. "Uh ... *P* ... *E* ... *B* ... *Z* ... *F*."

"Huh?" said Heather.

"Next line, dear," Nurse Patti nudged me.

I sighed and just read off the letters, completely giving up on answering the advice-off question. I was so glad the TV was in the other room. I didn't even want to know what messed-up horror-of-a-name Heather had written down.

The last three questions went about the same as the first two. By the end, Heather was so flustered that when asked "Can I swear skinny jeans with sneakers?," she wrote word-for-word what I told Nurse Patti about tripping over my own foot:

"Only a big dork would do that."

Although, to be honest, I probably would've said the same thing either way.

When the advice-off ended, there was no question who'd won. It was time to face the entire school.

And worse . . . Mary Patrick.

CHAPTER 10

Own It

I wished I could've hid in the nurse's office for the rest of the day, but after realizing there wasn't anything wrong with me, Nurse Patti sent me away so she could take care of a kid who'd sprained his wrist.

"Lucky," I muttered when I passed him.

"Have a pink and paisley day, dear!" Nurse Patti called after me.

I braced myself for what awaited in the halls after homeroom, and as soon as people saw me, the stares and whispers began. For some reason, it didn't make me embarrassed; it made me angry.

These people with their judgmental comments and pitying looks were the reason I had stage fright.

"I didn't visit the nurse for deafness," I said, cornering two girls I saw whispering. "I can hear all of you!"

"Oookay, let's not scare the villagers," said Brooke, dragging me away. "So . . ."

I sighed. "What?"

"Did that little scheme turn out exactly as you planned?" she asked.

I hung my head. "Did it look as bad live as it did on the TV in the nurse's office?"

"Worse, I think," said Brooke. "Because I could actually smell sweat and fear coming off Heather."

My stomach flipped. Heather, sweet Heather, who was so shy she wouldn't do a solo in choir, had embarrassed herself for me.

"Awww. I have to talk to her."

I turned toward the auditorium, but Brooke gripped my arm tighter.

"She'll be fine," she said. "Stefan took her to photograph some butterflies, and I'm pretty sure she's in love."

"With the butterflies or Stefan?" I asked, smiling.

"What you really need to worry about is Katie," continued Brooke. "She is mad."

I snorted. "Like I care. She's the reason I got into this mess in the first place. *And* she's going to win the advice-off, anyway. She should be happy."

Brooke wrinkled her forehead and glanced sideways at me. "Katie put a lot of work into promoting the advice-off, and you didn't thank her once."

"I didn't ask her to help," I retorted. "And trust me, she did it to promote herself, not the two of us."

A runty kid I didn't recognize stood at a nearby water fountain, just staring.

"What?!" I roared.

He squeaked and ran away.

"V, what has gotten into you?" asked Brooke. "Calm down."

"Everyone's staring at me!"

"Everyone's curious about what happened," said Brooke in a calm, quiet voice. "Just act like nothing's wrong, and they'll find something else to be nosy about."

I took a deep breath and stood tall, smiling at anyone who happened to look our way . . . which was everyone.

"Say something," I whispered to Brooke.

"Hi!" she told people, waving. "I hear the cafeteria's serving tuna!"

I jerked on her arm. "Say something to me!" I amended. "Act like we're talking."

"We are talking," she said.

"That's good. Tell me about . . . I don't know. You and Abel. Did you choose your costumes?"

"Well, I came up with an idea," she said non-committally.

"And?" I prompted. "Did Abel like it?"

Brooke squirmed. "I don't know. I haven't told him about it yet."

"Why not?"

"What if he doesn't like it?" she asked. "He and I already fight so much. I don't want to add to his 'Reasons to Break Up with Brooke' list."

I raised my eyebrow. "Is that a real thing?"

She shrugged. "I'm just guessing."

"Okay." I grabbed her arm and turned her to face me. "I need the real Brooke Jacobs to come out and play now."

She wrinkled her forehead. "What's that supposed to mean?"

"The Brooke I know is never afraid to speak her mind," I said. "And she knows that if someone doesn't like what she has to say, they can just move along."

Brooke stared at me for a moment, and I almost thought I had her, but then she crumpled and turned away. "But, V, he's cute and funny and smart!"

"There are lots of cute and funny boys out there, and if he's smart, he sees what's so great about you, just the way you are," I pointed out. "But if you start being a timid little mouse to keep him around, you're going to have to stay that way as long as you date him. Is Brooke Jacobs a timid little mouse?"

A familiar fire sparked in her eyes. "No!"

"Is Brooke Jacobs a fierce girl who knows what she wants?" I asked.

"Yes!" she said.

We slapped a high five, and she leaned over and hugged me. "Thanks, V. You're not too bad at this advice stuff." She backed away and winked. "When you show up."

The warning bell rang for first period, and she squeezed my arm. "You're on your own now. Don't kill anyone, don't choke anyone, and don't challenge anyone to a duel."

"You take all the fun out of middle school," I teased.

Even though Brooke had told me to act like nothing was different, it was harder to be as confident without her around. I ducked my head low and hurried to my first class.

The English teacher, Mr. Cummings, turned from the verbs he was writing on the whiteboard.

"Miss Jackson, glad to see you've recovered in time to make it to my class."

Several kids turned their attention to me, and I blushed.

"Um . . . yeah," I said. "Turns out it was one of those half hour bug things."

He smiled and continued to watch me as I stood nervously in the doorway.

"Waiting for the bug to come back?" he asked.

"Something really close," I said. "Is there any way I could skip class today?"

"And get a zero on the pop quiz? Sure!" he said in a cheerful voice.

I groaned. "There's going to be a pop quiz?"

"There might be if you leave," he said with a wink.

Clutching my purse to my chest, I made my way to my desk as quietly as I could.

Eyes flitted over to me and heads bowed in conversation. The guy who sat behind me tapped my shoulder. "Your illness isn't contagious, is it? Because I'm going to the Navy Pier this weekend."

I shook my head dumbly.

He narrowed his eyes. "Is it laryngitis?"

"No." I got out of my seat and walked to the pencil sharpener, turning my back to the class and grinding my pencil slowly down to a nub.

The last bell rang, and everyone shuffled to their seats but me.

"Miss Jackson?" Mr. Cummings said. "To your seat, please."

More whispering. More wondering. I couldn't take it anymore. I had to take the advice I'd given Brooke and own who I was.

I whirled around and blurted, "I have stage fright!"

Mr. Cummings blinked. "Well, luckily, we aren't onstage. Although Shakespeare would beg to differ."

I shook my head. "No, I mean earlier. That was why I wasn't at the advice-off. I have stage fright, and I didn't want to be on camera, and I'm sorry I didn't show up." I glanced around at the other kids.

The guy who sat behind me raised his hand. "Is that contagious?"

Several people laughed. I breathed a sigh of relief. Telling the truth hadn't been so bad.

"I would love it if you would all find *learning* contagious," said Mr. Cummings. "Miss Jackson, to your seat, please."

As soon as I sat down, Gabby, who sat across from me, leaned over and whispered, "I get stage fright too."

"Then our dream of being in a rock band will fail," I told her.

We giggled.

At the start of my next class, I did the same thing, admitting the truth about my stage fright. It was easier to deal with the truth than with people whispering rumors about why I hadn't shown up.

By lunchtime, I was actually smiling at the lunch lady. Until she reminded me of something.

"Did you see the advice-off this morning?" she asked, plopping a corn on the cob on my tray.

"That Katie is one cute, smart gal. She'd be perfect for my nephew."

I plodded to the lunch table with sagging shoulders.

"Why so glum, chum?" asked Heather.

"Katie's going to win the advice-off," I said.

"Unless you just came from an alternate universe where you actually showed up for the advice-off, then yes," said Tim. "Pudding?" He offered me a cup.

I took it, ripped off the lid, and poured pudding into my mouth.

"And you *definitely* won't be giving advice on manners," he said, eyebrows raised.

"I won't be giving advice on anything," I said with a heavy sigh. "Not for days."

"At least you'll have time to work on the drama club costumes," said Heather, putting an arm around me.

"Heather." I turned and gave her a big hug. "I

am so, so sorry about this morning. I'm a jerk."

"It's okay," she said, giving me a squeeze.

"I shouldn't have asked you to fill in," I said. "I should've had Tim do it."

"Yeahhh," he said, narrowing his eyes shrewdly. "That was the lesson to take away from all this. I'm going to get another pudding."

I stuck my tongue out at him and turned back to Heather. Since it was just us, I asked, "How are the Irish dancing lessons?"

She blew a raspberry and gave a thumbs-down. "Everyone in the class is about my *bubbe*'s age, and I feel out of place. I spend most of my time watching the other students to make sure nobody breaks a hip."

I willed myself not to laugh. "I'm sorry, Heather," I said. "Maybe—"

"V!" Brooke raced over to us, throwing down her lunch bag, which slid a good foot across the table. "The peanut butter cups! Where are they?"

She grabbed my shoulders.

"Huh? Uh . . . in my backpack," I said, bending over to get them.

"What's going on?" asked Heather.

"It's—"

I straightened, clutching the package to me. "Mary Patrick!"

Brooke nodded. "She's on a serious rampage in the newsroom to get rid of us and our column."

"I have to go talk to her!" I jumped to my feet, and Brooke immediately pushed me back down.

"Nooo. Do you recall making a little speech in any of your classes today?"

I nodded. "In all of them. I told them about my stage fright."

Brooke took the chocolates from me. "Well, that morphed into Mary Patrick forcing you onstage against your will while you begged and cried."

I clapped my hand over my mouth and shook my head.

Heather stood and picked up her lunch tray. "It's just a big misunderstanding. Tim and I will go talk to her."

She grabbed his arm as he was coming back to the table.

"But . . . my pudding," he said, holding it up.

"Save it," said Heather. "We may need it to fight off Mary Patrick."

"I'll be right behind you guys!" said Brooke, picking up her lunch bag.

"What should I do?" I asked.

"Mrs. H is having Gil cover the photo shoot at the estate tour. Apparently, Stefan had something come up. I told her you'd go with Gil, and she thought that'd be the best idea."

I picked up my backpack. "Where . . . ?"

"The group is leaving from the courtyard in five minutes," she said. "Go the long way, so you can skip the newsroom. Good luck!"

Brooke hurried after Tim and Heather.

I felt like a spy as I dropped off my tray, stole a glance over my shoulder, and slinked down the hall that ran parallel to the main one. At the front common area, I peeked around the corner and then raced out the front door to the courtyard.

I'd managed to escape the wrath of Mary Patrick. For now.

CHAPTER

11

One Moment in Time

A sea of students was milling around a row of school buses, slowly filing onto them in crooked lines. I spotted Gil at the end of one with a photography bag slung over each shoulder.

"Gil!" I called, waving.

"Hey, Vanessa!" He waved back. "What are you doing here?"

I tried to ignore the students looking at us while they waited to board. "Mrs. H sent me to help," I said, telling a quarter of the truth. "Want me to take a bag?"

"You . . . are my hero," he said, letting one slide

down his shoulder so I could grab it.

"I thought Stefan was going to take pictures of this tour," I said, adjusting the bag while we shuffled forward with the line.

"He had a better opportunity come up," said Gil with his easy smile. "But again, I'm not complaining!"

He stepped onto the bus, but a teacher at the front of the line stopped me from following.

"I don't recognize you," he said.

"She works for the paper," said someone behind me. "She's the girl Mary Patrick tried to force onstage for the advice-off."

"Oh," he said.

I turned. "Oh, no, she didn't—"

"Do you have a field trip waiver filed with the office?" asked the teacher.

"Yes," I said. "All the newspaper staffers had to get one. But what I was saying—"

The teacher jerked his head to one side. "Go

ahead and get on. Keep the line moving, people!"

I climbed onto the bus and took the seat next to Gil.

He must've overheard the earlier conversation because he said, "Did Mary Patrick—"

"No," I cut him off. "I just have really bad stage fright."

Gil chuckled. "That's wild. I'd never picture a girl like you being afraid of anything."

I cleared my throat. "So Tim told me about a photography exhibit that Stefan wants to enter," I said. "Are you going to enter too?"

"Changing the subject. Okay," said Gil, still grinning. "And no, I'm not entering."

"Why not?" I asked.

"I guess you could say I have my own version of stage fright," he said. And left it at that.

We rode for a while without talking, Gil drumming a beat on the seat in front of us with his fingers. The bus stopped in front of a tall narrow building that looked a little like a castle.

"They're going to tear this place down?" I asked, gazing out the window. "Why?"

"To make room for something bigger and newer," said the teacher who'd confronted me earlier. "People just don't appreciate the past anymore."

It took a while for everyone to get off the bus and into the old house, and when we walked through, we were led in groups by a tour guide. In one side room, there were two people in business suits sitting at a massive mahogany table that was cluttered with clocks and cups and random knickknacks.

"What's all that?" someone asked.

"The auction house is cataloguing items for the estate sale," said the tour guide. "If you'll follow me . . ."

As we walked, Gil snapped photos left and right.

I followed him up the steps. "How are the pictures looking?"

He laughed. "It's just like Stefan said. I'm taking pictures of an old house."

We finished our tour and were back on the bus fifteen minutes later. Gil showed me some of the pictures he took.

"These are great!" I said. "You should enter one of them in the exhibit."

"Maybe," he said thoughtfully. He squirmed in his seat, and in a voice that sounded almost shy said, "Want to see what I'd enter if I did?"

"Absolutely," I said.

Gil reached for his cell phone and shuffled through the pictures before turning the phone so I could see it.

The picture was of a red cart with a "Shave Ice" sign on its roof. The cart was surrounded by a fence of surfboards in all the colors of the rainbow, and a palm tree waving in the background.

"'Shave Ice'?" I asked.

"It's kind of like a snow cone. They're really popular in Hawaii, where my family's from," he said. "My parents had their first date here."

I held the phone closer. "You're from Hawaii?"

He nodded. "Well, I was born there, anyway. This was my parents' favorite place to go to with my older sisters, when they were young, but a couple months after they had me, they had to move to the mainland. We've only been back once, and that's when I took this photo." He took the phone back and looked at the picture. "A few days on the beach are all I know of the place where my life began."

"That's sad." I leaned over and hugged him. "I'm sorry! You should totally enter that photo in the exhibit."

"Nah," he said, putting his phone back into his pocket. "Nobody would understand."

"Sometimes I feel that way about fashion,"

I told him. "That people might not understand something I create, but I go ahead and do it anyway, because it makes me happy."

He nodded. "You're a Leo, aren't you? Your sign, I mean."

I regarded him with awe. "How'd you guess?"

"You have the traits," he said with a shrug. "Stubborn and proud."

"I will take those both as compliments," I told him.

Gil laughed. "And very optimistic."

I furrowed my brow at that one. "I don't know. I haven't been very optimistic lately. That advice-off kind of brought me down."

"It's one moment in time," he said with an amused look. "And it's not even a life-changing one, like a move from Hawaii to Illinois."

"Yeah. You got me beat on that one," I said with a grin.

"That's what photography is all about," he

said. "Catching a moment, a memory, that's worth preserving."

"Like the Ecklesby Estate," I said.

He nodded. "Exactly. You really think in ten years you'll look back on the advice-off as one of the biggest moments of your life?"

"The way I handled it? Definitely worth passing on to the grandchildren," I said with a laugh. "But if I'd actually been in the auditorium . . . no."

Gil held out his hands, as if to say, *See?*

"Well, at least consider submitting something," I said. "You've got skills."

"Thanks," he said, his old grin back.

My phone buzzed with a text message from Brooke that read:

It's safe to come back. Mary Patrick ate half a bag of chocolate, which has made her too happy and too full to chase you very far.

The bus pulled in front of the school, and Gil and I made our way to the newsroom. Mary

Patrick sat at a table strewn with Reese's wrappers, staring sullenly at me.

"Hi," I said, knocking softly. "I never said that you forced—"

"I believe you," she said, cutting me off. "But you embarrassed me and this newspaper."

Seeing that she was still calm, I took a seat across from her.

"I'm sorry," I said. "It didn't turn out the way I planned."

"Why didn't you tell me what was going on?" asked Mary Patrick.

I stared at my hands. "You were so gung-ho about the advice-off that I was afraid you'd force me to get onstage."

Mary Patrick sighed. "So there was a *little* truth to the rumors."

I pinched my fingers together. "This much."

She toyed with a wrapper. "I'll admit I can

be . . ." She struggled to come up with the word.

"Impossible?" I offered.

Her frown made it clear that wasn't the right word.

"Overzealous," she said. "Especially when it comes to the paper. But if I knew it upset you that much, I wouldn't have made you do it. We could've come up with something different. Like a prerecording. Or you could have just written down your answers beforehand, and I could've showed them on the air. You wouldn't have even had to be on camera."

My cheeks warmed with a blush. "Oh. I hadn't thought of that."

"You were probably too busy throwing away your pink and paisley shoes," she said. Then she smiled.

I smiled back. "I'm never going to live that down, am I?"

"No. In fact, I wouldn't be surprised if everyone comes in next week wearing fashions by Yigal Pebzfjanolk."

I giggled, and after a second, so did Mary Patrick.

When we stopped, she reached into the pile of wrappers and pulled out a still-intact Reese's cup, passing it to me.

"You know Katie's going to win," she told me.

"If she didn't, I'd question the intelligence of everyone in this school," I said, taking the candy she offered.

"I know you could've beat her," said Mary Patrick.

A lump formed in my throat, making it harder to swallow the chocolate.

"Thank you," I mumbled.

"I'd still like you to choose the questions she answers. I know you'll pick good ones."

I nodded and crumpled the foil. "I won't let you down."

Mary Patrick smiled. "I know. Have a good afternoon, Vanessa."

I got to my feet and picked up my book bag. "After this morning, it can only get better."

When Mom came to pick me up from school for my dentist appointment, there was a stuffed bear sitting in the passenger seat. It had on a pink, sequin-covered dress and ballet flats.

"I got your message," she told me. "And thought you could use a friend. I call her . . . Bearsace."

I smiled and reached past the bear to hug my mom.

"That bad, huh?" she asked, giving me a squeeze.

"I never want to do anything like that again."

I sniffled and wiped my eyes. Then I leaned back in the seat and picked up the stuffed animal. "It was almost too much to . . . bear."

One corner of my mouth curved up in a smile, and Mom beamed at me.

"There's my girl. Now tell me what happened."

One thing about my mom? She has the best laugh in the universe. As I started to tell her about the nurse's office and my various screwups, she laughed harder and harder until at one point she had to pull over and lean against the steering wheel.

Her amusement was infectious, and it wasn't long before I was having trouble talking from all the giggles that would take over.

"Oh, baby, I am so sorry," she said. "I know it's not funny, but . . . did you really say *Ahhhhh-mish* when Heather asked you who makes the best clothing?"

"I had a tongue depressor in my mouth!" I said

with a laugh. "And the Amish are really good at sewing, so I wasn't completely wrong."

Mom snort-laughed and pulled back onto the road. "You are too much."

By the time I left the dentist's office, I was feeling great, which most kids don't usually say. As soon as Mom pulled into our driveway I ran to my room with Bearsace under one arm.

And froze in the doorway.

"Oh," I said, holding the bear in front of me like a furry shield. "Hey."

I'd forgotten Katie was going to be sitting for my little brother. She was on the edge of my bed, with her legs crossed at the ankle, wearing a seashell necklace around her head like a crown and holding a plastic pitchfork. My brother was wearing a plastic breastplate and pointing a plastic sword at her. Battling the Mermaid.

"Hey yourself," said Katie. And without missing a beat, "I think you owe me an apology."

"Really?" I scoffed. "You think you earned one?" I prodded Terrell on the shoulder. "Go in the kitchen and ask Mom for a cookie."

"But we haven't finished!" he told me. "We're still fighting over the treasure."

"The treasure is yours. Congratulations," I told him, pushing him toward the door. "Go ask Mom for two cookies."

"Okay, okay," he said, pouting. Then he turned and waved with his sword arm. "Bye, Katie!"

She smiled and waved back. "Good-bye, brave warrior." As soon as Terrell was gone, her expression turned serious. "What was with that stunt you pulled, Vanny?" she asked. "I thought we were in this together."

I placed Bearsace on the dresser. "Uh . . . no. We were never in it together. You did everything without talking to me, even after you knew I had stage fright."

"I thought you got over it!" she said.

"With the *Learn French* videos you sent me?"

Katie winced. "Yeah, sorry about that."

"Wait." I stared at her. "You knew you did it, and you didn't say anything?" A realization hit me. "You did it all on purpose, didn't you?"

"I . . . What?" Katie blinked rapidly.

I didn't know why I didn't see it before. It all made sense. The flyers, the contests, the constant reminders about the advice-off. All to build my anxiety so I wouldn't be even a tiny threat to her winning.

"Out." I pointed to the door. "Out of my house. Now."

"Vanny, I can explain. . . ." She stood and backed away.

"Don't even play at being my friend." I pulled myself to my full height. "My life is off-limits to you."

"You're wrong," she said, retreating into the hallway. "I wasn't trying to make you look bad! I am your friend."

"Yeah, well, your dictionary must have a different definition of *friend*," I said, closing my bedroom door in her face.

I reached for my schoolbag and yanked out one of the drama costumes and my pincushion. After three failed attempts, I finally threaded a needle and began to sew, tugging harder on the stitches than I needed to.

In a couple minutes, there was a soft knock.

"Vanessa?" said my mother through the door. "Is everything okay?"

I opened it a crack. "Katie's a bad person," I told her. "Do not let her in our home anymore."

Then I closed the door and went back to sewing.

Unbelievable. She'd rigged the advice-off in her favor. She'd even tricked my friends. All so she could prove that she knew more about fashion and beauty than I did and make a name for herself at the school?

Well, two could play at that game.

I finished the costume I was working on and stuffed it into my book bag. Then I opened my closet and found my black trench coat and boots.

It was time for the return of Van Jackson.

The Return of Van Jackson

"Do I even want to know?" Mom asked Thursday morning when I came downstairs in my Van Jackson outfit.

"Darling, you are killing it in those heels," I told her, lowering my sunglasses to peer over the top of them.

"Nope," said Mom. "I don't want to know."

She ushered me toward the front door and called to my brother.

"Why are you dressed like a spy again?" Terrell asked as we got into the car.

"Not a spy, dear boy, a world-famous fashion

designer." I reached back and offered him my hand. "I'm Van Jackson. Charmed."

Terrell licked it. "I'm a puppy. Arf, arf!"

"Ugh!" I jerked back my hand and wiped it on my pants.

Mom sighed and drove into the street. "Please don't get yourself in trouble again, V."

I settled back in my seat. "You mustn't worry so, Mother, darling. You'll get wrinkles."

She let me out at school just as Brooke's mom was dropping her off. When she saw our car, Brooke hurried over, waving. But as soon as she saw my outfit, she stopped.

"Oh no," she said. "You're not—"

"Van Jackson, darling." I offered my limp-wristed hand. Under my breath, I added, "Don't actually kiss my hand. Terrell just licked it."

Brooke wrinkled her nose. "Why did you bring back Van Jackson? She got you into trouble last time."

"Because, sweetums, the people crave her, and you have to give the people what they want." I jumped up onto the edge of the fountain. "Friends!" I cried to the people milling about. "I may have missed the advice-off yesterday, but I'm here now to answer any of your questions. Brooke, I believe you had one?"

"Huh?" Brooke glanced up from where she'd been fiddling with her phone.

"A fashion question?" I raised an eyebrow at her.

"Oh! Uh . . . yeah. Can I wear sneakers with a dress?"

Everyone looked from her to me.

"Excellent question!" I said. "Yes, as long as they're lace-ups, with a solid color and low tread. Think Chuck Taylors."

"Really?" asked Brooke with wide, hopeful eyes. "Don't mess with me, V. I really will do it.

Abel asked me to brunch at his parents' country club."

I laughed a high, tinkling laugh and waved a lazy hand. "Of course, darling! And please. Call me Van Jackson." I held my arms open. "Any other questions?"

A girl ducked her head and raised her hand ever-so-slightly.

"Clever girl. You've come to the right place for advice!" I said. "What's your question?"

In a soft voice she asked, "When does Katie get here?"

Stupid Katie.

I kept my smile pasted on and spoke through my teeth. "Any other questions?"

"I actually have one," said another girl. "Do—"

"Sorry I'm tardy to the party, dolls!" chirped an annoyingly familiar voice. "Who wants free bracelets?"

Everyone turned away from Brooke and me to look at Katie.

"What . . ." was all I could say.

Katie propped her sunglasses on top of her head with one hand and held out a fistful of beaded bracelets in the other.

"Come and get 'em while they're still in style!"

Like a wave leaving the shore and being pulled back out to sea, the crowd surged toward Katie and her bracelets. Amid the throng of confusion, I could hear all kinds of questions about bracelets, then jewelry, then fashion in general.

"Unbelievable!" I said, throwing my hands in the air. "Brooke, we're leaving!" I snapped my fingers and speed-walked toward the building.

"V, can I really wear sneakers with a dress?" asked Brooke, following me into school.

We nearly collided with Heather in her choir robe.

"Shouldn't there be, like, twenty more of

you?" asked Brooke. "And halos?"

"Practice ran long this morning." Heather smiled and then noticed my outfit. "Van Jackson again? We seriously need to make rule number sixteen 'No more Van Jackson.'"

"Well, don't worry," I said. "Katie made sure it was short-lived this go-around."

Heather glanced at Brooke.

"She brought free bracelets for everyone," explained Brooke.

"Ooh, what kind of bracelets?" asked Heather. At a glare from me, she scowled. "I mean . . . that Katie's a monster! I'll show her!"

I sighed. "It's hard to believe you in your choir robe," I said. "But thanks for the effort."

The bell rang for the start of school, and Heather waved to us. "I'll see you guys later."

Brooke walked with me to homeroom. "I don't get what your big problem is with Katie. She seems nice enough."

"Brooke, she knew I had stage fright, but she insisted on making a big production of the advice-off, which made it worse."

"Because you told us you could get over your stage fright," said Brooke. "It's not her fault you didn't."

"Still," I said. "She should have talked to me first."

Brooke nodded. "I'll agree with that."

For some reason, I didn't really feel like I'd won my case, though.

We took our seats in homeroom, and a girl next to me held up her wrist with a smile. "Thanks, Vanessa."

"Sorry?" I asked.

"For the bracelet." She pointed to the beads around her wrist. Katie's beads. "They're so adorbs!"

"You're . . . welcome?" I said, looking at Brooke.

She shrugged. "Don't look at me."

The girl opened her notebook, and I leaned over to tap her arm.

"Katie Kestler gave you that bracelet, right?" I asked.

She nodded.

"Then why are you thanking me?"

The girl smiled. "She said it was a gift from both of you."

I leaned back in my seat. So Katie was trying to make nice now. Well, too little, too late.

In Journalism, the bell rang just as Tim dove through the doorway.

"Very dramatic," said Brooke as he lay sprawled on the floor.

"Hey," he said, panting, "I can't . . . afford . . . another tardy."

Mary Patrick walked over to our area. "So we have the results of the advice-off," she said. "Two of you won, and two of you didn't."

All of us froze in our tracks.

"Two?" repeated Tim. "I thought Vanessa was the only one who screwed up."

"Thank you," I said.

"So which ones of us didn't make it?" asked Heather.

Mary Patrick pulled out a piece of paper.

"In the sports and fitness category, Brooke collected sixty percent of the votes, and Ryan forty percent."

Tim, Heather, and I clapped, but Brooke wrinkled her forehead.

"Only sixty?" she asked.

"Most guys are going to vote for another guy, whether he makes sense or not," said Tim.

Brooke narrowed her eyes. "Did you vote for me?"

"Of course!" he said. "I'm not most guys."

"Keep going," I told Mary Patrick.

"In the male perspective category, Tim

collected seventy percent of the votes, and Luke thirty percent."

"Yes!" Tim pumped his fist.

Brooke put a hand on his arm and lowered it. "Which means—"

Mary Patrick nodded. "Heather and Vanessa lost. Sorry." She gave us sympathetic smiles.

Heather's face was emotionless. "What was the final tally?"

"Yours was forty-five percent to her fifty-five percent," Mary Patrick told her, "and Vanessa—"

"Stop!" I held up my hand. "It'll be some huge and humiliating difference like zero percent to her one hundred percent."

Mary Patrick shook her head. "No. It's five percent to her ninety-five percent."

I gave Mary Patrick a big fake smile. "Oh, that's *much* better."

"Even though your competitors will be writing the advice, I talked to Mrs. H, and we agreed that the two of you should choose the questions, okay?" asked Mary Patrick. "Then we'll pass them along to Katie and Misha."

Heather and I both nodded.

"And let's do our best advice column this week, to remind our readers why they chose you"—she pointed to Brooke and Tim—"and why they should've chosen you"—she pointed to Heather and me.

"Well, that was something unexpected," said Tim as Mary Patrick walked away.

Brooke put her arm around Heather. "You okay?"

Instead of bursting into tears, Heather actually smiled.

"Forty-five percent!" she said. "I almost beat someone who works with the school counselor, you guys." She held up her hand for a high five.

"Hear, hear!" Brooke and Tim smacked it. "Now, let's talk about what we're putting in the column this week. Tim, how's your rap coming?"

Tim talked, and I leaned closer to Heather.

"Where's my high five?" she asked.

I patted her palm softly. "You're not upset about losing?"

"No," she whispered. "I mean, sure, I'm a little bummed, but just because Misha's good at it, doesn't mean I'm not. It doesn't make my advice any less valuable."

She turned so she could hear what Tim was telling Brooke, but I didn't join in.

Could what she said be true for me, too?

Just because Katie was being asked to speak in classrooms and had her own website and won the advice-off, didn't mean I wasn't great at fashion, and it didn't make my work any less valuable. She wasn't better; she was just different.

I sat up a little taller in my seat, and a happy glow bounced around inside me, warming every part it touched. When Brooke and Heather laughed at Tim's advice rap, I joined in, and that afternoon, when I was in the auditorium fitting actors for costumes, I didn't even flinch when Katie walked in.

Because the world was big enough for both of us.

CHAPTER

Stolen Treasures

"You seem to be in a better mood," said Mom.

I was sitting in the passenger seat, humming and looking at my friends' online social pages—Heather's in particular.

"I've decided I'm a pretty good fashion designer," I said. "Even if nobody else thinks so."

Mom raised her eyebrows. "Well, I'm glad you believe in yourself, but what makes you think other people don't?"

"Lately, everyone's been ignoring me and paying attention to Katie."

"That's because she's new, honey. And she's

from California, which is more glamorous than Illinois."

I giggled. "Yeah, I know. But they've also been going to her for fashion advice when they used to come to me."

Mom turned into our driveway. "Maybe because they've heard your advice before, and they've never heard hers. Did you think about that?"

I hadn't. And it made me feel even better.

"You're pretty smart for a mom, you know that?" I asked.

"They teach us just what to say in Mom 101," she told me with a wink. "They also teach us to say this." She shut off the car and faced me. "I am very proud of whoever you turn out to be."

I gave her a dubious look. "Even if I turn out to be a hook-handed psycho?"

She grabbed my nose. "Only for Halloween!"

I leaned in and gave her a hug, and she kissed the top of my head.

"Speaking of Halloween," she said, "you haven't shown me your costume since you started. I'd love to see how it's coming along."

"Oh, it's gorgeous!" I said. "You're going to love it."

I ran into the house, throwing my bag onto the bedroom floor and pulling my costume out of the closet. When I brought it to the living room, Mom whistled and clapped her hands.

"Very nice, honey! I think I can retire off the money you make being a designer."

I grinned. "I know the red on the vest doesn't match the brown-and-white stripes in the skirt, but the red in the choker brings it all together."

Mom tilted her head to one side. "What choker?"

"Huh?" I spun the dress to face me.

The strip of velvet with the dangling cameo, my grandmother's cameo, was gone.

"Well, it *was* on. . . ." I retraced my steps from the living room, into my bedroom, and into my closet.

Nothing.

I narrowed my eyes. Only one person who'd seen my costume had been in my bedroom when I wasn't there.

Katie.

I ran down the hall and threw open the front door.

"Where are you going?" asked Mom.

"To get my choker back from the thief who stole it!"

I hunched my shoulders and charged across the street, fists clenched at my sides. I raised one of them and pounded on the Kestlers' front door.

A curly-haired woman in a yoga outfit answered.

"Well, hi, stranger! I'm guessing you're Vanessa. Although if I know who you are, that doesn't exactly make you a stranger, does it?" She giggled and held out a hand. "I'm Katie's mom."

"Hi, Mrs. Kestler." I shook her hand. "Is—"

"Pleeease! Call me Bobbi!" She scrunched up her face and pointed her thumbs at herself. "I'm just one of the cool kids."

I closed my eyes and took a deep breath. "Fine . . . Bobbi. Is Katie home?"

"Oh . . . waaait." She leaned back into the house and cupped her hand around her ear, giving me an openmouthed smile. "I think I might hear her right now. Katie Bear, is that you? Your friend Vanny's here."

I groaned quietly. Like mother, like daughter.

"She is?" I heard Katie ask. A second later she appeared. "What's up?"

Bobbi was still standing right there, so I cleared my throat and said, "Can you please return that choker I let you borrow?"

Katie squinted. "Sorry?"

Bobbi let out an airy laugh. "I think she's trying to speak to you in code while I'm here. Message received." Bobbi gave me an exaggerated wink and disappeared into the house.

"What's this about?" asked Katie, stepping outside and closing the door.

"The choker on my Halloween costume. It's gone."

Katie balked. "And you think *I* took it?"

"Look," I said. "I can accept that you won the advice-off. I can accept that kids are coming to you for advice now. But when you try and steal my friends, steal my ideas, steal my alter egos, steal my spotlight, and now physically steal *from* me? That is taking it too far." I held out my hand, palm up. "Give it back."

She stood there, openmouthed, face turning

redder by the minute. At least she had the decency to—

Katie slapped my hand away. "How *dare* you!"

I blinked at her. "Excuse me?"

"No, I don't think I will. You don't deserve it." Katie pointed a finger in my face. "When I first moved here, I thought you were so amazing and wonderful and fun, and I wanted so much to be like you, and for you to like me. I tried to get in good with your friends, I tried doing the kinds of things you like to do. I tried to be your friend."

Katie's eyes were filling with tears, and her words were getting harder to understand. "But nothing I do is good enough for you. Not even these stupid friendship bracelets!" She took one of the bracelets she'd been handing out that morning and slid it off her wrist, slamming it to the ground. "I didn't steal your stupid choker, and I don't care if you ever like me because I . . .

HATE . . . YOU!" Katie roared the last words, spun on her heel, and stormed back into her house.

The door slammed so hard I felt my whole body shake. Or maybe it was shaking for a different reason.

"Vanessa?" Mom called from across the street. "Come here, please."

Great. She'd heard me and Katie fighting and was going to scold me. I crossed the street and walked into my house.

"Yes, Mom?" I said in my sweetest, most well-behaved voice.

Her expression was stern, but instead of hollering at me, she pushed my little brother forward. "Tell her what you did, Terrell."

Head bowed, my little brother held out his hand. Dangling from his fingers was the choker.

My body refused to move, frozen in utter shock. "*You* had it?"

"He took it when he and Katie were playing in your room," said Mom. "Isn't that right?" She nudged him.

He crossed his arms and glowered at her. "I was battling the mermaid, and I needed a treasure."

I finally reached for it. "But that means . . ."

I put my head in my hands.

"Vanessa?" Mom put a hand on my shoulder. "What's wrong?"

I shook my head. "Mom, I just did the most terrible, horrible . . ."

She pulled me onto the couch, and I told her what had just happened.

"Oh, Vanessa." The disappointment on her face was almost too much to bear. "You have to go fix this."

"You're right!" I ran back across the street, choker in hand, and banged on Katie's door again.

Bobbi answered again, but this time she wasn't smiling.

"Can I talk to Katie? I was wrong about something, and I want to apologize." I held up the choker as proof.

"I'm sorry, kiddo, but she doesn't want to talk to you right now. Maybe give her a few days?" Without waiting for my answer, Bobbi closed the door in my face.

I pulled out my cell phone and looked for Katie's number, which she'd programmed into my phone as "Cali BFF."

"How could I be so dumb?" I punched the number, but the phone went straight to voice mail.

"Hey, Katie, it's me," I said. "Uh . . . Vanny. I wanted to say I'm sorry. I found the choker. You were right. I was a bad friend. I didn't realize you were doing those things to get me to like you. I thought you were doing those things to . . . to be better than me." I sighed and walked back to my house. "Anyway, I'm sorry, and I hope you can forgive me."

I hung up and called Heather, telling her what happened. "What do I do?"

"Aww, V, I don't think there's anything you *can* do right now," she said. "Just give Katie some time to cool off and try not to torture yourself, okay?"

"Okay," I said. But I didn't follow her advice.

I tossed and turned all night, thinking of how I'd been treating Katie and what she'd said and all the things she'd done to prove we were friends. This new girl in town who I'd treated as an enemy.

The next morning, I got up extra early, so I could catch Katie when she left her house, but she never came outside, and eventually, Mom told me we had to leave or I'd be late.

Brooke and Tim were waiting by the curb for

me when Mom dropped me off.

"Heather told us what happened," said Brooke. "Did Katie accept your apology?"

I shook my head. "She's avoiding me."

"Write her a note," said Tim. "And have Heather give it to her before homeroom. She won't be rude to Heather."

"Good idea!" I sat on the edge of the fountain and took out my spiral. "What should I say?"

"'Dear Katie, you need to get over this,'" said Tim. "'I've already apologized, and I don't have time to tiptoe around your feelings.'"

"Wow." I frowned up at him. "No."

"Yeah, that's too mean," said Brooke. "How about 'Hey, buddy! My bad! Friends?'"

I twirled my pen between my fingers. "Too impersonal."

"'My dearest Katie,'" said Tim, holding the back of his hand to his forehead. "'Truly, I have been vexed since—'"

I pushed him. "I need to convince her not to be mad at me."

"You could give her a gift card," said Brooke.

"What, and bribe her to be my friend? No," I said. "She should accept me the way I am. I just made a mistake in judgment. It happens all the time."

"Yeah, the captain of the *Titanic* probably said the same thing," said Tim.

I clapped my hands together. "Focus, people! How do I get Katie to forgive me?"

But they'd gone to a silly place.

"You could mix wolf hair with unicorn spit and cast a spell on her," said Tim.

"You could find a magic lamp and make a wish," said Brooke.

"You could hire a plane to write a message in the sky."

"Guys!" I shouted so loud that they both jumped. "I need real solutions here."

Brooke shrugged. "There's no easy answer. She'll forgive you when she's ready."

"Yeah. Give it time," said Tim. "And if she isn't willing to forgive you, she isn't worth having as a friend, anyway."

Brooke bumped him with her elbow. "Hey, that was really good friendship advice! Heather would be proud."

It *was* good advice, and it was what Heather told me when I caught up with her outside her homeroom.

"You can write her a note, and I'll give it to her," she said, "but you can't make people feel the way you want them to."

"Are you sure?" I asked. "Even with a gift card?"

Heather smiled. "Yes, V."

I wrote a quick note, anyway, and handed it to her, but by the time Journalism rolled around, Heather didn't have anything to tell me.

"I gave her the note," she said with a shrug. "It's up to her now."

"Well, thanks for trying," I said.

Heather squeezed my arm and went to the front of the classroom to talk to Mary Patrick.

I went to my desk, and Gil swiveled in his seat to face me. "What are you doing tomorrow night?"

I stepped back in surprise. "Friday? Uh . . . nothing. Why?" I asked.

With a dramatic flourish, he presented me with a strip of paper.

"Mr. Gil Pendleton, your entry has been confirmed in the Berryville Civic Center . . ." A grin slowly spread across my face. "You entered your photo in the exhibit!" I jumped up and down, clapping.

"Want to see a sneak preview?" he asked.

"Only *of course!*" I said, stumbling over my chair to get to him.

"You okay?" asked Gil, helping me up. "It's good, but it's not worth face-planting over."

I stood, cheeks blazing, and dusted off my clothes. "I will be the judge of that."

Gil reached into his binder and pulled out a glossy page with two images on it. One, brightly lit, was the picture of the shave-ice cart in Hawaii. The other, in shadow, was the Ecklesby Estate.

"I love it," I declared. "A beginning and an end."

He nodded and high-fived me. "You totally get it. Will you come to the show?"

"I am absolutely there," I said. "Give me the details."

As if he'd been waiting for that response, he produced the event brochure.

I read over it. "Uh . . . not that it's any of my business, but what are you going to wear?"

Gil blinked and then shrugged. "Jeans and . . ."

He sniffed his T-shirt. "Probably this. It's my best shirt."

"*That's* your best . . . ?" I stopped myself. "Gil, this is an art show, not a pool party. People are going to be looking at you as much as your work."

He spread his arms open. "So? Let them look. This is who I am."

"You're putting in zero effort," I said. "You can still show them who you are and not get turned away at the front door."

He narrowed his eyes. "I don't like where this is headed. Please don't clap your hands and squeal, *Makeover!*"

I crossed my heart with my index finger. "All I'm going to do is see if I can find a different shirt that's a little classier and shows off who you are. I'll even message you a photo before I buy it."

Gil rolled his eyes. "Fine."

"Yay!" I lifted my hands and froze when Gil

raised his eyebrow. "I was only going to clap once," I said.

He grinned and gave me his cell phone number. Then he reached for his wallet, taking out a twenty. "Here. I can't have you buying stuff for me. It's unchivalrous."

I gently pushed his hand back toward him. "If I find the right shirt, then you can pay me back."

Mrs. H called for the start of class, and I went back to my desk, more gracefully this time. As she called each section, Mary Patrick got progress reports from everyone, and the topic of the advice-off came up again.

"I know it's only one week, but I'm going to miss answering letters," said Heather with a sigh.

I leaned my head on her shoulder. "How about I bring a bunch of magazines and some lawn chairs, and while everyone else is busy working, we can sit around and read?"

She giggled. "Can we drink smoothies out of tall glasses with umbrellas?"

"Out of *pineapples* with umbrellas," I told her.

"Don't forget," said Brooke, "you're still choosing the questions Misha and Katie are answering."

Tim left the room and came back with the latest advice requests.

"'Dear Lincoln's Letters,'" he read, "'What outfits will look good with my new braces?'" He passed me the paper. "I don't need to know fashion to answer that one. . . . Nothing."

I took the paper from him and saw that it didn't stop at just that question.

> Dear Lincoln's Letters,
> What outfits will look good with my new braces? I hate them, and I look weird. Is there anything that will make them (or me) invisible?
> Metal Mouth

"Awww," I said out loud with a frown. "I know I'm supposed to be choosing questions for Katie, but I *have* to answer this one."

"What one?" Katie appeared next to me.

I screamed.

Everyone stared.

Katie took a step back. "Sorry, I thought you saw me." She glanced around. "Sorry, everyone!"

"V, are you okay?" asked Heather.

I clutched a hand to my chest. "Katie, where . . . where did you come from?"

She pointed to the door.

"No, I know that," I said. "But . . . why are you here?" I took an excited breath. "Did you get my note? Do you forgive me?"

Katie shook her head. "Mrs. H thought it might be nice for me and the girl who's subbing for Heather to sit in and watch you guys work." She nodded to Misha, who'd stopped to talk to someone. "She got permission from our teachers for us to take ten minutes."

My shoulders dropped. "So you don't forgive me."

There was an awkward silence. She glanced at my friends.

Heather got to her feet. "Uh . . . hey, Tim and Brooke! Let's go sharpen our pencils!"

"I write with a pen," said Tim, holding it up.

"I want to watch them fight," said Brooke, staring at me and Katie.

Heather reached down and grabbed them both by an ear. "Pencil sharpening. Now."

"Owww!" said Brooke, getting up. "What are they *teaching* you in choir?"

"Yeah, and aren't you in Model United Nations?" asked Tim, following her. "This is *not* a peaceful resolution. Ireland would be ashamed!"

Katie watched them go and shook her head to get the craziness out. "Anyway," she said. "I can forgive you, but I can't forget what you did,

Vanessa. That was a ton of hurtful accusations that I didn't deserve."

I reached out for her hands. "I *know*," I said. "And I'm sorry. I was intimidated by you because you've got it all."

"Got *what* all?" asked Katie.

"Magazines interviewing you and stores wanting to see your fashions," I said, ticking off on my fingers. "Business cards and a website and—"

"And I'm still not getting any sales!" she said. "People don't want to back a twelve-year-old girl. They think because I'm a kid that I can't be taken seriously." She brushed her hair out of her face in an angry swipe.

"Oh." I pressed my lips together. "I didn't know that."

"If you had asked, you would've," she said. "I would've told you anything you wanted to know, but you chose to jump to conclusions and ruin a perfectly good friendship." Her voice deepened, but she didn't cry. "And now I have *no* friends at this school."

Just when I thought I couldn't feel worse . . .

"Katie—," I began.

She sighed and got to her feet. "I'm gonna go. Just . . . have your teacher email me whatever advice questions you want me to answer, okay?"

I twisted my hands together. "There's nothing I can do to change your mind?"

Katie turned. "It would have to be something huge."

"I'll work on it," I told her. "I really will."

It was too promising a friendship not to.

CHAPTER

14

Showtime

"I cannot believe I agreed to take you to the mall when there's a *House Hunters* marathon on," said Mom, swerving our van around a car waiting for a parking spot. "I must be out of my mind."

"Out of your mind with love for your daughter, yes," I said. "And I promised Gil I'd find him something."

"*I didn't!*" she said.

"Me neither," piped up Terrell from the backseat.

Mom pulled into a parking spot, and a few

minutes later we were in the department store.

"Okay, we don't have a lot of time," I said, "so start looking for something that says surfer/poet/hippie/drummer."

Mom just stared at me. "You're kidding."

"What about these?" asked Terrell, pointing to a rack.

"Those are Spider-Man pajamas," I said. "Not really Gil's style."

"I meant for me," said Terrell.

"Would you please focus?" I asked. "We're looking for a long-sleeve shirt that a poet might wear to a fancy party."

Mom and I started sifting through racks while Terrell engaged in a battle with the hanging Spider-Man pajamas.

"What about this?" asked Mom, holding up a baggy linen tunic.

"That's what a *medieval* poet would wear to a fancy party," I said. "Think modern."

"How about this?" She pointed out a button-down shirt with flowers.

"Think masculine."

"This?" She held up a T-shirt with fake muscles printed on it.

"You're hilarious."

"Honey, fashion isn't my forte," said Mom. "And I've never met this Gil boy, so I have no idea what he's into."

Nevertheless, she kept on looking, and after a while Terrell tried to help too. Some of the things they chose made me cringe, while others made me laugh. And I started to realize how awesome my family was to be doing something they disliked, just to help me. The great thing was, I probably could've called in Brooke, Heather, or Tim, too, and it would've been just as much fun.

Despite everything Katie had going for her, she didn't have these wonderful people in her life the way I had them. She might get close with my friends, but it would never be the same as *my* friendship with them because her personality was different than mine. There was no way I could be Katie Kestler, because then I couldn't be Vanessa Jackson.

"My last attempt," said Mom, holding up a striped long-sleeve crewneck with a solid chest pocket.

"That . . . is actually perfect," I said, taking it from her.

"Really?" Mom looked pleased with herself. "Look at me, I'm a hip mom."

"I wouldn't go *that* far," I said, and ducked out of her reach before she could grab me. I snapped a pic of it and texted it to Gil, who sent me back a smiley.

When I got home, I worked all the way up until bedtime, adding a special touch to the shirt, and on Friday in Journalism, I presented it to Gil.

"Vanessa! This is awesome!" He ran his fingers over the special touch: stitching of a surfboard. "But I don't remember seeing this in the picture you sent."

"I put that on myself," I told him. "So now the shirt is customized just for you."

He beamed, lovely dimples reappearing. "I feel like I owe you more than just the twenty dollars this cost," he said, handing over the money.

"That smile," I told him, "is extra payment enough."

While the news team put last-minute touches on their work to meet deadline, I kept glancing at the classroom door, wondering if Katie might come in to watch us.

She didn't.

That evening, Gil and his parents showed up to take me to the civic center, and I gave him two thumbs-up when he met me at my front door. "That shirt is so you!"

"Is it? I'm not very sure about anything right now," he said.

I called good-bye to Mom and walked with Gil down my driveway. "You'll do fine," I assured him as we walked to his parents' car. "You don't have to speak or anything, do you?"

He shook his head. "But that's not what I'm worried about. What if nobody likes my entry?"

"*I* like it," I told him firmly. "And if you want, I can stand next to it all night and ooh and aah over it."

Gil chuckled. "You don't have to make any sounds, but I wouldn't mind the support."

I greeted Gil's parents and asked them about life in Hawaii. Gil leaned back in his seat and relaxed with a smile on his face.

"I love thinking about that place," he said.

Gil's dad dropped us off in front of the civic center, and his mom led the way to the registration table.

We walked into the display hall, which had buffet tables set up in the center, piled high with fruits and cheeses. Along the walls were easels featuring the photo entries.

Gil bumped my shoulder and pointed with a grin. "There's mine on the end!"

He hurried toward it, and I pulled out my cell phone. "Stand next to it and let me get a picture," I said.

Gil posed, and I raised my cell phone just as a strong hand clamped down on my shoulder.

"No photos of the art, miss," said a man in a security uniform.

Why was I always in trouble with them?

"You should have a sign. . . ." I trailed off when I realized I was standing right next to one. In fact, they were posted every few yards. "Oh. Sorry. We don't want to take pictures of all the exhibits. This one is my friend's." I pointed to the display.

The security guard shrugged. "Sorry, but I don't make the rules. She does." He pointed to an old lady with a pinched face.

When she saw us looking, she narrowed her eyes.

"Well, what about them?" asked Gil, pointing to some people at the entrance with a video camera dragging cables behind it.

"They're with the local news," said the security guard. "They've got permission. Excuse me."

He trotted off to stop some other people with their own camera at the ready.

"Well, that sucks," said Gil.

"But you're going to be on the news!" I told him. "Look, look, here they come!"

I backed up to get out of the path of the news crew as they approached, but the cameraman stopped just to the left of Gil's photos and then crossed the room to film the other side.

Gil and I watched him go.

"That was rude," I said.

"I guess he didn't want us in the footage," said Gil with a shrug.

More people began wandering into the room, and I tugged on Gil's arm.

"Let's get some food before it's all gone."

We stood where we could see Gil's photos and gauge audience reaction.

Some people paused and pointed to the Ecklesby Estate, no doubt chatting about its soon-to-be demolition. Others just stared from the image of Hawaii to the image of the estate, as if confused by what it could mean.

"Just out of curiosity, what did you name the exhibit?" I asked Gil.

"Name?" he repeated.

"You know . . . how artists name a painting so people can understand what they're expressing," I said. "Like van Gogh's *Starry Night*."

Gil raised an eyebrow. "You never cease to

amaze me. I wouldn't see you as an art buff."

I blushed. "Well, I don't know the names of *all* the great works, but art and fashion design are kind of the same. You start with an idea, jot some things down on paper, and bring it to life."

"Like writing books," said a voice next to me. "Seriously, how can you not appreciate them more?"

I rolled my eyes and turned to face Tim. "*What* are you doing here?"

"I appreciate art in *all* its forms," he said, gazing down his nose at me. "What are you doing here?"

"Gil entered the exhibit, and I'm here to support him," I said. "To stay by his side no matter what."

A couple approached Gil's exhibit, and I pushed him toward them. "Go!"

"Hey!" He dug in his heels. "What are you doing?"

"Stand by your exhibit and talk about it," I told him.

Gil tugged on the bottom of his shirt to straighten it and approached the couple, rubbing his hands together.

"He looks like he's trying to start a fire," said Tim. "Are you sure he's going to be okay on his own?"

"He'll be fine," I said.

Except he wasn't. As soon as he started explaining his photos, the couple wandered away.

"Rude," I said with a frown.

A man in a pinstripe suit strolled by and stopped to look at the photos. Gil tried his speech again, but as soon as he'd said one word, the man looked him up and down and kept on strolling.

"Hey!" I said.

Tim shushed me. "People don't have to like the photographs."

"But they don't have to be rude to the photographer," I said.

Poor Gil was shifting from one foot to another, shoulders hunched, staring at the carpet.

"Hey, look, a camera crew," said Tim. "And they're coming this way!"

"Yeah, they've been by here already," I said, glancing over. But this time a woman with a microphone was with them. "Oh, this is perfect! She can interview Gil."

I waved to get his attention and pointed out the reporter. Then I pulled myself to my full height. Gil nodded and did the same, standing next to his exhibit with his hands behind his back.

The reporter strolled sideways while she held the microphone and talked at the camera.

"They're almost here!" I whispered, clutching Tim's wrist.

"For someone who gets stage fright, you're

alarmingly excited," he said.

"That's because . . . Wait—" The camera once again stopped right before it reached Gil. The reporter started walking back from where she came, still talking.

Gil's mouth opened and closed, but he seemed at a loss for words.

I sure wasn't.

"Hey," I said, hurrying after the news crew. "Why are you ignoring my friend?"

They didn't hear me.

"Hey!" I said again. "HEY!"

The cameraman and reporter jumped and turned around in alarm. So did everyone else in the room.

"You missed a great exhibit on the end," I said, pointing at Gil's. "Why don't you want it on the news?" I looked at the cameraman.

Tim cleared his throat. "Uh . . . V?"

"Is it because a kid submitted it and you don't

think it's worthy?" I continued.

"V . . . ," said Tim.

"Let me tell *you* something"—I pointed my finger at the reporter—"my friend's work is amazing and meaningful. It's about where life begins and where it ends. It's special to him, but you act like it doesn't matter."

She raised her eyebrows. "You seem very passionate about this."

That's when I noticed she was holding the microphone out to me. And that the camera's light was blinking.

I was on TV.

I froze for just a second, but then I saw Gil out of the corner of my eye, watching me with a hopeful expression.

I nodded and took a deep breath, keeping my eyes on the woman. "Just because we're younger, people treat us like we don't know anything, like we've never experienced life," I said. "But we've felt emotions, and we've seen beauty, and we know what we like. Take my friend Katie Kestler . . ." I stopped. "Well, my former friend Katie Kestler. I kind of ruined things by—"

Tim prodded me in the back.

I looked at him. "Right. Not the point." I faced the reporter. "Anyway, Katie is a brilliant fashion designer, and she's smart and professional, but because she's only twelve, nobody takes her seriously. And nobody takes Gil seriously." I pointed to him, and the camera panned over.

Gil's eyes widened, and he waved nervously.

"Could you please just film maybe five seconds of his photo entry?" I asked the cameraman.

"No, he may *not*," said a woman's voice. "And I shall tell you why."

Everyone, including the cameraman, turned toward the old woman with the pinched face who I'd seen earlier.

"I have specifically requested that exhibit

not be filmed because it will belong to *me*." She gestured to Gil. "If, of course, you are willing to sell it."

Gil squeaked. I translated. "You want to buy his work?" I asked.

The old woman laughed airily. "Don't sound so surprised. Weren't you just praising its merits?"

"Well, yes," I said. "But . . ." There wasn't anything to argue. I grinned. "Yes, ma'am."

The camera swiveled back to the reporter, who smiled broadly and said, "Ladies and gentlemen, the people have spoken *and* been heard. A photographer was noticed for being a talent, not a teen. This is Allison Delaney reporting live from the civic center for Channel Five News."

The light on the camera stopped blinking, and the cameraman lowered it to his side. The reporter turned and extended her hand to me.

"Thank you for turning a boring news

segment into something delightful," she said.

I shook her hand, and then she waved to Gil. "Best of luck to you."

"Thank you!" he said.

As soon as she walked away, Gil hurried over and high-fived me and Tim.

"Holy cow, can you believe it?" he asked, laughing. "I never in a million years would've guessed today would turn out this way."

"Yeah, I don't think Stefan did either," said Tim, nodding toward the opposite side of the room.

Our lead photographer stood scowling with his arms crossed next to a photo of himself with his arms crossed.

"I think they call that a self-fulfilling prophecy," Tim added.

The three of us snickered.

"Vanessa." Gil held his arms open to me.

"Thank you for talking me into doing this. And for convincing me to wear a different shirt."

I laughed and leaned into his bear hug. "You're welcome. I'm glad you were brave enough to try the exhibit *and* the shirt."

"I hate to ask," said Gil, stepping back, "but would you be okay if I disappeared for a bit? My parents are talking to the woman who wants to buy my work."

Tim nudged my arm. "My dad and I can give you a ride home if you need one."

"Thanks." I nodded and smiled at Gil. "You're off the hook!"

He grinned his dimply grin. "I'll call you tomorrow and tell you how it went." He waved to me and Tim and then trotted off.

"He couldn't see this coming in a million years," I told Tim, "yet he writes our horoscopes section."

Tim snorted. "I told you those things are bogus. So, are you going to tell Brooke and Heather about your moment in the spotlight?"

"Actually," I said with a grin, "I think I'm going to let them watch it for themselves."

CHAPTER

15

Trip or Treat

I t was incredibly hard to keep everything a secret, but luckily, or unluckily, I had Katie to preoccupy my mind. Only a grand gesture would convince her to be my friend again. What could I do?

When I got to Heather's soon-to-be-haunted house for Musketeer Movies, I asked her the same thing, but only after promising not to walk past the front sitting room. The TV had been rolled in on a cart, and there were already drinks and boxes of Chinese food waiting for us.

"The props and decorations for the party

are spread all over the rest of the house," she explained. "I want it to be a surprise."

"Got it," I said with a wink. "Now about Katie . . ."

"A grand gesture . . ." Heather plopped down on a couch. "Do you have any connections in the fashion industry that can get her career going?"

I raised an eyebrow. "If I did, you don't think I'd use them myself?"

She nodded. "Fair point. Does she have a dying family member?"

I made a face. "Geez, I hope not! Why?"

"Well, a grand gesture could be to support her during a time of crisis." She held up a finger. "But don't create a time of crisis."

"Please. I'm not Brooke," I told her.

"Good to know there's only one of me," said Brooke from the doorway.

"Hi!" Heather greeted her. "Don't go any farther than this room."

She glanced at the curtained-off entrance to the dining room. "Dragons?"

Heather shrugged. "You never know."

"What are we talking about?" asked Brooke, settling down to pour herself a soda.

"Huge gestures that V can do to convince Katie to be her friend," said Heather.

Brooke nodded and slurped up the fizz at the top of her cup. "Just make sure that whatever you do doesn't affect the advice column."

I made a face. "You sound like Mary Patrick."

"It *is* almost Halloween," she said. "How do you know I'm not her in disguise?" Brooke wiggled her eyebrows.

"Since we're all here," I said, pulling out my phone. "I wanted to show you guys something that I saw on the news last night."

Brooke and Heather stared in confusion but moved in on either side of me as I pulled up Channel Five's video links.

"The news?" asked Brooke. "You're not eighty."

I grinned and turned up the volume. "Just watch."

An image of the civic center appeared on the screen.

"Oh, the photo exhibit that Gil entered!" said Heather. "Is he on here?"

Brooke shushed her, and the three of us sat in silence as Allison Delaney from Channel Five News appeared in front of a row of exhibits.

My heart pounded as she walked and the camera followed, stopping just to the left of Gil. The camera turned away, and then . . .

"AAAAAAAH!" Brooke and Heather screamed the minute I appeared on-screen.

Totally worth the wait.

I paused the video and held up my arms. "Ta-da!"

"V! You're on TV!" cried Heather, pointing repeatedly at the screen.

"How did you . . ." Brooke gaped at me. "You're terrified of cameras! What were you doing there?"

"Watch." I unpaused the playback, and the recorded version of me asked, "Why don't you want it on the news?"

In the background, recorded Tim said, "Uh . . . V?"

Brooke and Heather squealed. "Tim!"

I put a finger to my lips, and we all listened to my impassioned speech. When I glanced at Brooke and Heather, they were leaning forward, hanging on every word. As soon as the reporter signed off, Brooke hug-tackled me.

"I'm so proud of you!" she shrieked. "You got over your stage fright."

Heather, who'd managed to calm down a bit, waited for Brooke to back away before giving me a hug of her own.

"I'm proud of you too," she said with a squeeze.

"And as for a grand gesture to Katie? I'm pretty sure *that* was it." She nodded to my phone.

My jaw dropped. "I didn't even think about that! It was, wasn't it?"

Brooke hooted. "Oh yeah. If Katie can't forgive you after you promoted her on the five o'clock news . . ."

"V was on the five o'clock news!" cheered Heather.

The excitement was overwhelming. "Woohoo!" I leaped off the couch and punched the air.

"And she jumped off furniture and didn't hurt herself!" added Brooke.

"*And* since I'm full of surprises today . . ." I reached into my bag and pulled out a receipt, handing it to Heather.

"What's that?" asked Brooke, craning her neck to see.

"A favor for Heather, since she did such a huge favor for me during the advice-off."

Heather stared at the receipt. "A week of Irish folk dance lessons . . ." She gave me a confused look.

"I joined your class, lassie!" I said with a wink.

Heather gasped and hugged me again. "Yay!"

Brooke still looked lost. "What class?"

I made a face. "Oops. I forgot that was supposed to be a secret!" I shrugged at Heather. "Sorry."

She waved away my apology. "It's fine. Are you really coming with me?"

"Of course! It's the least I can do," I said.

Brooke stamped her foot. "What is happening?!"

Heather blushed and told Brooke her surprise for the Halloween party.

"I know it's silly," she said. "But I'm really trying to immerse myself in the culture."

"I think it's great," Brooke assured her. "Have you learned any moves yet?"

"A couple," Heather admitted. Then she stood and stepped back a few paces to demonstrate.

"That looks so cool," I said as she shifted from foot to foot.

Brooke stood next to Heather and watched her movements, trying to imitate her.

I burst out laughing. "You look like you stepped in something that you're flinging across the room."

Brooke beckoned me over. "Let's see you try."

I joined in on Heather's other side and gave it my best shot. From the snorts of laughter all three of us made, I definitely wasn't any better.

The following afternoon, I went with Heather to her step-dancing class as promised and also enjoyed being a minor celebrity on the internet . . . in a good way. The news footage of me and Gil was quickly making its way around my classmates' social media. By Monday morning, the link address was even taped up in Locker

411 with an accompanying note: *A star is born!*

So I was deeply confused when Katie refused to meet my eye every time I passed her in the hall. And I made it a point to pass her a lot.

"How can she still be mad at me?" I asked my friends at lunch.

"At this point, I'd say her loss." Tim waved a dismissive hand. "You put in more than enough effort."

Brooke and Heather agreed, and to keep my mind off it, I went with Heather to another step dancing practice that afternoon. While we were waiting for her mom to pick us up, Heather asked, "I know it's last minute, but can you help me work on my costume?"

I looked up from the boot I was lacing. "I thought Katie was doing that."

Heather shrugged. "She told me something came up. And we were almost done!"

I shook my head. "There's something wrong

with that girl. But sure, I'll help."

Heather's costume and the dance lessons were a good distraction for both of us, since we weren't getting to work on the advice column. Every day that week, I was tempted to ask Mary Patrick if I could read what Katie had turned in, but something told me that snooping wouldn't be the best way to get back on Katie's good side. Even though Tim said I should just move on, I still kind of hoped we'd be friends again.

Finally, finally, it was Saturday, and time for the Schwartzes' Halloween party!

Mom dropped me off in front of their house, which was nestled in a sea of fog. Gravestones were scattered all over the front yard, and an owl with glowing yellow eyes watched us from a tree.

"Oh my," she said. "The Schwartzes went all out."

I opened the car door. "Yeah, they always—"

"BRAIIINS!" A bloodied zombie popped out from behind the tree, and I leaped back into the car with a shriek.

The zombie doubled over laughing. I realized it was Heather's oldest brother, Max.

"Are you going to be okay in there, honey?" Mom asked me with an amused look.

"If I can make it to the front door," I said, clutching my heart.

Max knocked on the car window. "Come on out. I won't eat you. . . ." With a fiendish grin he added, "Yet."

I glanced back at Mom, as if it might be the last time I ever saw her. "If I die, bury me in Prada."

She blew me a kiss, and I climbed out of the car.

Max pointed toward the garage. "Stop by the funeral parlor first and get your photo taken in the coffin. The later it gets, the more crowded it gets. You might say"—he paused—"people are *dying* to get in there."

Despite myself, I snort-laughed at his joke. "That was terrible."

"There's plenty more where that came from." He winked at me and disappeared behind the tree to terrify the next partygoer.

"Vanessa Jackson!" Heather's dad, dressed like a vampire, greeted me as I approached the garage. "Lovely to see you, dear. And what a pretty costume!"

He helped a guy dressed like a ninja into the coffin.

"Hi, Mr. Schwartz. Thanks! This place looks awesome." I gestured at the decorations.

"We've had many years to perfect it," he told me with a wink.

A guy in pirate garb stood over the coffin and took a picture of the "dead" ninja.

A door inside the garage opened, and a blast

of music came out, along with Heather, wearing her Irish folk dancing costume.

"Daddy, Mom wants to know where you put—" She stopped when she saw me, and waved. "Hi, V! You look so cute!"

I hurried over and hugged her. "You, too!"

"Well, I had an excellent tailor," she said with a smile. "Are you going to get in the coffin?" she asked as the ninja stepped out.

"You only live once, right?" I handed her my purse and stepped into the coffin.

"Cross your wrists and lay your palms against your chest," Mr. Schwartz said, demonstrating.

I did as he said, closing my eyes until I heard the camera click.

"Are Brooke and Tim here?" I asked Heather, letting the pirate help me to my feet.

"Tim's not here yet, but Brooke is," she said. Then she smiled. "And I invited Gil, too."

"You did?" I said, smoothing down my skirt

and touching my hair. "Is he here? Do I look okay?"

"Aye, ye be lookin' like a treasure!" said the pirate.

I did a double take. "Gil?"

I blushed, realizing he'd just seen me get flustered over him, and tried to play it cool.

"I mean . . . dude! Boss threads!" I said in my best surfer voice, punching him in the shoulder.

He simply smiled. "Nice save."

I blushed some more and giggled. "I like your costume. It's definitely a good disguise."

"And I like yours," he said. "It's definitely you."

"She made it herself!" chimed in Heather.

"I wouldn't expect anything less," said Gil.

"Come on, let's go inside." Heather grabbed us both by an arm. "Daddy, can you take pictures for a while?" She shot him a meaningful glance, and he chuckled.

"You can *count* on me," he said, pointing to his costume. "Get it? Because I'm Count Dracula?"

Heather rolled her eyes but smiled. "Daddy, you need a new costume and new jokes. Oh! And Mom wanted to know where the Mice Cubes for the Pest Punch were."

"The freezer," he said, taking the camera from Gil. "But make sure people know not to eat them. I need a lawsuit like I need a hole in the head."

"Come on!" Heather tugged us toward the door, where the music grew louder.

Inside, paper lanterns shaped like black cats and white ghosts were strung across the ceiling, and all the inside lighting had been replaced with orange bulbs. Spiderwebs gathered at every corner, and white curtains over the windows were covered in spatters of fake blood.

A dozen or so costumed kids milled around the living room, chatting or standing by the snack tables, sampling foods labeled with signs like "HamBOO!gers" and "Devil Eggs."

"You have to try the Pest Punch," said Heather. "I made it myself!"

On our way to the drinks table, we almost collided with a guy in a deerstalker hat and cape.

"Oh, sorry!" I said. Then I squinted at him. "Brooke?"

"Well spotted, my dear Jackson." Brooke held a magnifying glass up to her eye. "And I deduce that your costume is exceptional!"

I curtsied. "Thank you! I thought Abel wanted you to go as something girly," I said.

She winked at me. "There was a change of plans. Isn't that right, Watson?" She stepped aside so I could see Abel.

He was wearing a butler's uniform. "Quite," he said, with a cheesy grin.

"Wait. The guy who founded Young Sherlocks has to play Watson?" Heather asked.

"We're gonna switch costumes halfway

through the party," Brooke assured her. "The Case of the Stolen Identity. I guarantee nobody else at the party is doing it. We might even win the contest!"

"I was skeptical at first," admitted Abel. "But it's actually a clever plan. And you know Brooke can be pretty persuasive."

He put an arm around her, and she winked at me. The real Brooke had prevailed.

"I still don't get it. How is he Watson, exactly?" asked Gil.

"I'm in disguise," said Abel. "Red herring?"

He held out a tray with a single strip of dried fish on it.

On the other side of them, someone else laughed. "I see what you did there. Nice."

It was Tim, wearing a suit of armor with a fake horse strapped around his middle. In one hand he held a lance made out of a poster tube.

"Who are you supposed to be?" asked Brooke.

"Don Quixote, the gentleman from La Mancha and professional windmill slayer." He bowed over his horse.

"I think you might be out of luck with windmills," I said. "There aren't any around here."

"Or have I already slain them all?" Tim twisted his mustache deviously. Then he leaned closer. "Actually, Gabby has a windmill costume, and I get to attack her with no parental consequences." In a louder voice he added, "But now, I must away to find food for my trusty steed!"

He trotted off, lance lowered to part the crowd.

The rest of us looked at one another and laughed.

"Excuse me, guys, I have to tell my mom about the Mice Cubes." Heather slipped past us and disappeared into the kitchen, the entrance of which was covered with yellow police tape.

Gil nudged me. "Would you like a glass of punch?" he asked.

"Sure," I said.

Abel turned to Brooke, who nodded, and the guys headed off together.

Brooke faced me and smiled. "So as you can see, things with Abel are going better. And it looks like you and Gil . . . ?" She let it trail off.

I just grinned. "No clue what's going to happen. I'm just gonna go with the flow."

She nodded. "Laid-back sounds like the perfect approach for him." Then she looked me over. "I know I said this earlier, but I love the costume!"

"Thanks! I'm not sure how long I'll be able to wear these shoes, though. They're already killing my feet." I lifted one of my legs so she could see the Mary Janes I was wearing.

"Oh, I guarantee there's no way your feet are

hurting as bad as Katie's," said Brooke.

Instantly, my stomach dropped into my toe-crushing Mary Janes. "She's here?"

Brooke beckoned for me to follow, and we worked our way across the room, which was getting more crowded, waving to kids we knew and stopping every now and then to talk costumes with someone. Finally, we reached the corner of the room where a werewolf, a fairy, and Thor sat on folding chairs next to Katie. She was leaning back in an armchair, dressed as a mermaid in a completely enclosed tail.

When she saw me, she instantly got to her feet, but because of her tail, she lurched forward, swinging her arms wildly.

Brooke and I cringed, but Thor caught her by the arm just before she hit the floor.

"Thanks," she told him, giving one more wobble before she found her bearings. She turned to me and Brooke. "Hey."

I elbowed Brooke. "Why don't you help the guys get the punch?"

She sighed and walked off. "I never get to stay for the fun."

Once she left, I returned Katie's greeting. "Hey. I love your costume."

She nodded. "Thanks. Yours turned out pretty good, too." She cleared her throat. "Okay, better than pretty good. Awesome."

I gave her a small smile. "So . . ."

There was a shout, and two guys stumbled into me, one of them sending a cup full of Pest Punch flying all over my costume.

My beautiful. Handmade. Costume.

I looked down at the damage and gasped, taking in deep gulps of air while trying not to cry. Katie stared at me, wide-eyed and frozen.

And then she reached out for me.

"Oh, Vanny! Oh, it's okay. We'll fix it. Shhh."

"But . . . but . . ." I fanned my face.

"Don't cry!" She pointed to one of the guys. "You! Get me some seltzer water and paper towels. Now!"

The guy gave us a befuddled look but ran off, and Katie squeezed my hand. "I've got a stain-removing pen in my purse. I'll be right back!"

But she forgot about her tail and flopped forward, landing on her hands and knees.

"Shoot!" she said, lifting the bottom of her costume so she could move her feet. It didn't help much since her costume still bound her legs together. All she could do was shuffle forward on the tips of her toes.

It was the funniest thing I'd seen since Mr. Llama ate the candy bar.

And suddenly, the tears turned into laughter.

Katie glanced back in confusion. "Vanessa?"

"Your mermaid walk!" I demonstrated her movements and laughed even harder.

"Hey!" she said. "This is a very serious"—she

giggled—"fashion . . . emergency."

We both doubled over, laughing, Katie holding on to me to keep her balance.

Heather ran over, bottle of water and paper towels in hand. "Is everything okay?" She slowed when she saw us laughing.

I nodded and giggled, taking the cleaning materials from her and sitting on an empty folding chair to work on my dress. "Thanks, Heather."

"I'll be close by if you need anything else." Heather smiled and left Katie and me alone.

Katie wiped tears of laughter from her eyes and hiked her dress up to knee-level so she could walk normally to her purse. When she came back with a tiny stain-removing pen, I waved it away.

"Thanks, but this dress is a goner," I said with a sigh. "There's no way that pen has enough in it to get all this out."

"I'm sorry, Vanny," said Katie, putting the cap back on the pen. "About . . . well, everything."

I looked up from where I was rubbing at a dark spot. "You are? Even though it was my fault?"

She sat down next to me. "It wasn't entirely your fault. I might have pushed too hard."

"Only because you wanted the best for me," I said.

"And because I wanted to be your friend," she said. "I thought you were amazing." She corrected herself. "You *are* amazing. I mean, the five o'clock news?"

I grinned. "You saw that, huh?"

"How could I not? It was everywhere!" She opened her arms wide. "You were so brave to get in front of the camera to support kids like us, and you were sweet to mention me by name. I wish I'd known beforehand. I could've given you a promotional T-shirt to put on!" Katie shook her head. "What am I thinking, T-shirts aren't fashionable. I could've given you a promotional scarf to wear!"

I cleared my throat, and she smiled sheepishly. "Yep, I heard it. I'm doing it again."

"So, if you were so happy about what I did, why have you been avoiding me?" I asked.

"I felt like a jerk," she said, jabbing the capped end of the pen into her leg. "I couldn't even finish Heather's costume, I was so distracted. Vanessa, I'm sorry we were fighting. Can we be friends again?"

"Well . . . I've never been friends with a mermaid," I teased. "But I think I'd like that."

Katie and I hugged.

Gil strolled over with two cups of punch. "Is everything okay? Heather told me you'd been punched."

I laughed and took one of the cups. "Something like that."

"Are you in the middle of something, or do you want to bob for eyeballs with us?" he asked, pointing to Brooke, Abel, Heather, and Tim.

"I'd love to," I said, getting to my feet. "But only if Katie can come."

I offered her my hand, and she took it with a smile.

The three guys ended up bobbing for fake eyeballs while we watched, along with the rest of the crowd. When people happened to glance our way, Katie would wave to them.

"You like the costumes? They're handmade! KV Fashions!" she called.

"KV Fashions?" I repeated.

She shrugged. "Doesn't hurt to try it out. And if we trademark it now, nobody else can use it!"

I laughed and shook my head. "You're too much."

Abel ended up collecting the most eyeballs and winning a music gift card. Then the overhead lights dimmed and a spotlight shone in front of the Schwartzes' fireplace, where an elevated stage had been set up.

"Ladies and gentlemen," Mr. Schwartz's voice boomed over a microphone, "the costume contest is about to begin!"

There was a buzz of excited chatter as people crowded around the fireplace to watch or walk the stage.

Katie nudged me. "I know you braved the camera, but are you prepared to get in the spotlight?"

"Of course!" I said, striking a pose. "I'm Vanessa Jackson."

And this was the night I'd been waiting for.

Dear Metal Mouth,

A lot of kids get embarrassed about their braces, but it's really no big deal. Why? Because the braces come off! Who cares what other people think? You'll have a great smile in a year, and they'll have a lousy personality forever.

As much as I talk about fashion and looking good, it's even more important to love what you've got going on inside. Be proud of who you are because what you have to offer is different from everyone else. (I mean, how boring would it be if red was the only color? Although, it IS universally flattering.)

Vive la différénce!

Confidentially yours,

Vanessa Jackson

Acknowledgments

Always for family, friends, and God.

For Justin McNeely, who never fails to answer a plot distress call with a brilliant idea.

For Nikki Loftin, whose twisted humor and laugh amuse me to no end.

For Carolina Aponte, who always talks from the purest part of her heart.

For Jen Hibbard, who tells me what I need to hear, not what I want to hear.

For the Society of Children's Book Writers and Illustrators, who helped me get my career off the ground.

For Deena Lipomi, who I rarely see but have

some of the best conversations with. Move to Austin already!

For Mark Moore, a great boss and a great man, whose amusement at my zany life matches my own.

For the Bellemares, who always watch out for me and turn cringe-worthy moments into laugh-out-loud ones.

And for Cheri Williams and Rachel Marks, who I adore because they make me laugh, despite having feet.

In case you missed the first book in this fun new series, read on for a sneak peek of:

BROOKE'S NOT-SO-PERFECT PLAN

1

The Three Musketeers

Look, I'll show you how to juggle the soccer ball *one* last time," I told Vanessa. "I can't watch you hit yourself in the face again."

"To be fair, I thought we'd be using our hands," she said, rubbing her nose. "And juggling something softer . . . like puppies." A bright pink spot stood out against her skin. If *I'd* been smacked with a soccer ball that many times, my entire face would be as red as my hair.

I tightened my ponytail and took a few steps backward on the school's front lawn. "I'm going to bounce the ball from foot to foot to knee to chest"—I pointed to myself—"and then deflect it to you to hit with your head." I pointed to her. "Got it?"

Vanessa made a face. "Why did I agree to this?" she asked.

"You said you had first-day jitters," I reminded her, balancing the ball on the top of my head. "And the best way to get over them is by distracting your brain. Ready?"

"As I'll ever be," she said, dropping into a squat. Not so graceful for a girl in a wrap skirt, but my fashionista best friend never seemed to care what other people thought. "Come on, Brooke!" she urged me. "School's about to start."

At those words, my arms broke out in goose bumps. Vanessa's jitters had jumped to me . . . but who could blame either of us? This was our first day as middle schoolers!

I shivered with excitement and dropped the ball onto my foot. With the flick of an ankle, it bounced to the other foot, where I popped the ball up waist-high. From there I bounced it on my knee and then leaned back to catch it on my chest. I deflected the ball off me and straight to Vanessa.

Who caught it with her right eye.

"Owww!" She clapped a hand over the side of her face.

"Oh my gosh!" I ran to her. "Are you okay?"

Several kids getting off a bus stopped to stare.

"Theater auditions!" I called to them. "*Ow: The Musical.*"

Vanessa lowered her hand and blinked up at me. "How bad is it?"

"Well . . ." I winced. "Are eye patches in style by any chance?"

She stared at me for a moment and then burst out laughing.

One of the things I love about my best friend? Nothing keeps her down.

"I don't know how you do it, Brooke," she said, rubbing her face. "Soccer's hard . . . especially the ball."

"Awww." I hugged her. "Sorry. I guess I'm just used to it."

"Used to it" was putting it mildly. I've been playing since first grade, and last year I even joined a traveling team, the Berryville Strikers. We came really close to the state championship. This year, that title's ours!

"Maybe you should see the nurse before homeroom," I told Vanessa. "Your face is covered with splotches now."

"Not a problem," she said, reaching into her backpack. She pulled out a slick black case and snapped it open. It was full of eye shadows, blushes, and bronzers.

"I still can't believe your mom agreed to let you wear makeup," I remarked. "You must be the only twelve-year-old in eyeliner."

"I'm pretty sure she got sick of me stealing her stuff," Vanessa said with a grin.

Grabbing a thin makeup brush, she dabbed it in a few colors and swept it across the red spots on her skin. In a matter of seconds, her face was an even mocha tone.

"Amazing."

"I'm still gonna get some ice from the nurse, though," she said, studying her reflection. "I don't want to start middle school as a one-eyed freak."

"At least you'd be on the front page of the *Lincoln Log*," I teased her.

The *Lincoln Log* was our school newspaper . . . one that Vanessa; our other best friend, Heather Schwartz; and I would be working on in our Journalism elective class. We were hoping to get "the Three Musketeers"—our nickname from elementary school—as a byline.

"Don't you dare put me on the front page!"

Vanessa said, narrowing her eyes. She quickly shifted to a smile. "I'd rather be in the style section."

We walked under a giant stone arch with "Abraham Lincoln Middle School" carved into it and stopped just outside the front doors.

"This is it!" said Vanessa with a broad, toothy smile and a nervous bounce. "Sixth grade!"

I nodded and grinned back. "Big things are going to happen for us this year. I can feel it."

"Let the adventure . . . begin!" She pushed on the door.

It didn't budge.

"I think you have to pull," I said.

"Oh." Vanessa yanked on the door handle. "Let the adventure begin!" she repeated.

A rush of unfamiliar sounds, smells, and sights attacked my senses. I tried to find something or someone I recognized while Vanessa hooked her arm through mine.

"Everyone's so tall," she whispered, gazing up.

"Maybe we don't drink enough milk," I mumbled back. I opened my binder and pulled out a campus map, but Vanessa immediately slapped it out of my hand.

"Don't let them see that! They'll think we're tourists!"

I shot her a confused look. "Huh?"

She shook her head and picked up my map. "Sorry, it's something my mom says when we're in Chicago. Defensive reflex."

I found the nurse's office on the map, and Vanessa and I braved the crowd in the hallways, stopping just outside the nurse's door.

"Save me a seat in homeroom!" Vanessa called as I walked away.

"I probably don't have to!" I shouted back with a grin.

Any time a teacher sat us by last name, it was almost guaranteed that Brooke Jacobs would be sitting behind Vanessa Jackson. The only thing missing?

"Heather!" I called, spotting her outside the music hall. No surprise, considering she's in choir. Vanessa and I are always begging her to sing our favorite songs because her voice is amazing. Like, pop-star-meets-angel amazing.

Heather smiled and waved at me, then went back to her conversation with another dark-haired girl, Gabby Antonides.

I darted through the crowd to join them.

"Hey, guys!"

"Hey!" Heather's voice was soft but excited. "Can you believe we're finally here?"

"No more elementary school. No more pee puddles from the kindergarteners," I said.

Heather giggled. "Or first graders crying when the lights go out."

"Ha! You think it stops there?" asked Gabby. "My brother's still afraid of the dark."

Heather and I laughed.

Gabby's twin brother, Tim, was a giant and a jock. Not exactly the kind of guy you'd expect to need a nightlight.

"So how was your summer?" I asked Gabby.

She rolled her eyes. "Good and bad. I met this cute boy at camp—"

"Good!" I gave a thumbs-up.

"But I kind of lied and said I was the most popular girl in school."

"Bad." I gave a thumbs-down.

"And it turns out he lives in Berryville."

"Worse." I used the thumb to cut off my head.

"Oh, stop," said Heather, bumping me with her hip. "You're scaring Gabby." She took our friend's hands. "You guys don't even go to the same school, so it may never come up. But if it does, tell him the truth and apologize. Say that you were nervous and wanted to impress him."

Gabby's expression grew anxious. "You don't

think he'll hate me?"

"No," Heather said firmly. "There is too much nice about you to hate."

Gabby beamed and hugged her. "I should get going." She waved at us and then ran off.

"I'll never have your knack with people," I told Heather. "But you probably knew that after . . ." I repeated the head-slicing gesture.

She smiled, but held it back just enough to keep her teeth from showing.

Heather is pixie cute but really self-conscious about this teensy-tinesy gap between her front teeth. Vanessa and I have secretly made it our goal to get real smiles out of her all the time.

"First day of school!" I said, trying again.

All Heather did was squeal and grab my hands. "Where's Vanessa?" Heather stood on her tiptoes to peer over the crowd. "She should be with us for this!"

"She went to the nurse's office," I said. "Soccer

ball to the face. Many times."

Heather sighed and shook her head. "That girl needs to design herself a Bubble Wrap wardrobe."

The bell rang, and Heather and I faced each other with wide, excited eyes.

"It's time," I said. "The start of middle school!"

Heather squeezed my hands and squealed again. "Good luck! See you in Journalism!"

"Watch out for hungry eighth graders!" I told her, and darted off to find my homeroom.

Since each grade has its own hallway, it wasn't too hard to find. Plus, our homeroom teacher, Ms. Maxwell, had tacked a huge sign outside her door that said, "Welcome, F through J!"

She was standing in the classroom's entrance with an armful of packets, handing one to each student who entered.

"Good morning!" she said when I stepped closer. "Name?"

"Brooke Jacobs," I said.

"Welcome to Lincoln Middle School, Brooke!" She handed me a packet. "And here is your middle-school survival kit."

"What's inside?" I asked, feeling the weight of it.

"Just some tips about getting the most out of middle school, important dates and room numbers, and information about this year's clubs."

"Clubs? Awesome!" I glanced past her into the classroom. "Um . . . where do I sit?"

Ms. Maxwell held her arms open. "Anywhere you want!"

I staked out two desks in the corner and threw my bag on one of them for Vanessa. After saying a few hellos to the kids I knew, I opened my packet and pulled out the club sheet and a pen, poring over the list.

"Hey! Whatcha doing?" asked Vanessa. She slid into the desk behind me with a wet towel over half her face.

"I'm choosing clubs. What's this about?" I lifted the corner of the towel.

"I'm using a cold compress to reduce swelling," she said. "What clubs are you looking at?"

I handed her the page, and she whistled. "Dang, girl. You circled almost all of these! Art, athletics, band, cooking—"

"I'm hoping they'll let us make pizza."

Pizza is my favorite, pepperoni in particular, and should, in my opinion, be its own food group.

Vanessa kept reading all the way to the end. "Young Sherlocks?"

"I think I'm pretty good at solving mysteries," I said. "Remember that smell in my bedroom? Finally found the source."

She wrinkled her nose. "Well, I, for one, am sticking to whatever will further my fashion career." She frowned. "Which is absolutely nothing on this list."

"What about theater?" I asked. "You could help with costumes and makeup."

Her eyes lit up. "Ooh. Good point!"

I scanned the list. "And Model UN is probably going to want flags or outfits to represent the different countries. Like . . . those overalls and pointy hats for Germany."

"Um . . ." Vanessa wrinkled her forehead. "I'm pretty sure people wear suits for UN meetings."

"Really?" I raised my eyebrows. "I always pictured it like It's a Small World at Disney. How disappointing."

The rest of homeroom and my morning classes (math, PE, and English) went pretty much like elementary school, except with different teachers for each one. And, horror of horrors, homework on the very first day!

At the end of English, every kid in my class scrambled for the cafeteria and our first taste of freedom: lunch. All of sixth grade ate at the same time, while the upper classes ate in later shifts. Probably to spare the sixth graders from ending up in the trash cans.

I found my two best friends, and we claimed a table by the ice-cream cart.

"Middle school is *hard*, you guys," Heather said with a groan. She was in all advanced classes. "In science we're already prepping for our first lab."

"Ooooh, what are you doing?" asked Vanessa. "Building a better human?"

Heather smiled at that. "I think we're smashing rocks."

"Too bad," said Vanessa. "Because my classes are seriously lacking in cute guys." She leaned closer. "I think it's so we'll pay more attention."

Heather giggled. "Could be. But I've seen some pretty cute ones in the older grades. Like Stefan Marshall?"

"And Abel Hart," I added. "But we're also

seriously lacking good PE teachers. I need to keep fit for soccer, and an hour of dodgeball isn't exercise!"

"Even though your soccer skills probably make you really good at it," said Heather with a smirk.

"Actually . . . the opposite," I said. "I'm so used to kicking anything that comes at me that I was out in the first two minutes."

Vanessa and Heather looked at each other and then burst out laughing.

"It's not funny!" I said, fighting back a smile.

"So what you really meant," said Vanessa, "was that *watching* an hour of dodgeball isn't exercise."

"Quiet, you!" I threw a grape at her. She deflected it, and it landed in Heather's pudding.

"Hey! I was going to eat that!"

"Like you can't sacrifice one thing on your tray?" I asked, eyeing Heather's lunch of tuna salad, chips, fruit, pasta, and cake. For a tiny girl, she can seriously chow down. I'm pretty sure she has extra stomachs, like a cow.

We chatted and ate until the bell rang. There was a massive groan from the entire lunchroom, followed by a scraping of chairs on linoleum.

"Journalism time!" I chirped. "*Lincoln Log*, here we come!"

"Save me a seat," said Heather. "I have to get rid of some chocolate pudding that somehow made its way onto my shirt." She narrowed her eyes at Vanessa.

"I'll help," she said with a sheepish grin.

I ventured to class alone, expecting the newsroom to be packed with students, shouting about deadlines and brainstorming ideas. But when I got there, I was only the third person to show.

In the front row a blond girl scribbled like mad in a notebook. Two rows behind her a guy sat with one long leg resting on top of the desk and the other in the aisle, tapping a beat with his foot.

The girl looked way too frantic to approach, but the guy was doodling a lion, the symbol for Chelsea Football Club, my favorite soccer team. I took it as a sign and sat beside him.

"Chelsea?" I asked.

He blinked at me. "No, I'm Gil."

I laughed. "I meant are you a fan of Chelsea Football Club?" I pointed to his drawing.

"Ohhh!" He laughed too. "No, it's Leo. You know . . . the zodiac sign? I do the horoscopes." Then he returned to his drawing and started bobbing his head to imaginary music.

I settled back in my seat and looked at the white-board while more students strolled in. Different sections and jobs at the paper had been written on the board with names beside them: *editor in chief, features, sports, entertainment, opinion . . .*

I frowned. All the positions were filled. What

was left for the Three Musketeers?

"Hey!" said Vanessa, dropping into the seat on my other side. "Why the long face?"

I pointed to the board. "What are we going to do? Everything's taken."

Heather took an empty seat in front of us. "Don't worry! We'll find something that's perfect for us. It's like my mom always says—"

"Hey! Sixth graders!"

All three of us snapped our heads around to look for the speaker. The blond girl who had been writing up a storm was now shaking her head with disapproval and pointing to the front of the classroom.

The teacher, Mrs. Higginbotham, waved at us. "Let's do a quick roll call before we get started, shall we?" She glanced at a clipboard and then up at the class. "Tim Antonides?"

"Oh, yay!" I said, looking around with everyone else.

On top of being Gabby's brother, Tim had played in a coed baseball league with me. He was fun to talk sports with, mainly because he didn't end each sentence by spitting, like the other guys.

But I didn't see Tim, and he didn't answer.

Mrs. Higginbotham called his name again before moving on. As students responded to the roll call, she jotted their names on a seating chart.

"Welcome to Journalism," she said when she was done taking attendance. "I see a lot of familiar faces and some new ones, but any input is always welcome. This class is an elective, but you'll still be graded based on your contribution to the newspaper. Our first issue will be what we call 'the short issue,' since the school year starts on a Wednesday and we don't have an entire week's worth of news yet. Nevertheless, I expect the sections to have their pieces in by Friday, and I expect quality material."

The blond girl raised her hand and stood to

face the class before Mrs. Higginbotham could say another word.

"Greetings, everyone," the girl said with a tight smile and curt nod. "My name is Mary Patrick Stephens, editor in chief of the *Lincoln Log*."

Her tone made it sound as if she were president of the United States.

"Since it's my final year with the paper, I want it to be a great one. This means brilliant stories and hard-hitting journalism." She pounded a fist into her hand. "Articles that would make Woodward and Bernstein proud!"

Vanessa leaned toward me. "What do woodwinds and Burt's Bees have to do with anything?"

I put my finger to my lips.

Mary Patrick spun toward Mrs. Higginbotham, blond hair fanning out around her shoulders. "You can count on this journalism team, Mrs. H. We will not let you down!"

Mrs. Higginbotham regarded her with wide

eyes. "Th-thank you, Mary Patrick. You can be seated."

"She's a little intense," Heather whispered over her shoulder.

I nodded, but deep down, I admired Mary Patrick's commitment to the paper. It was like me, with soccer. I'd practice as long and hard as it took to be the best.

Mrs. Higginbotham clapped her hands and looked at the rest of us. "As I said, the short issue is due Friday for release next Monday. I don't want you to worry about layout yet; I'm more concerned with content. Most of you know your jobs, but we have half a page that needs to be filled." She sighed. "Zack's still on probation for his article 'No Pants Day.'"

Several people giggled, but nobody volunteered to write for the half page. My hand shot up.

Mrs. Higginbotham pointed to me and

glanced at her seating chart. "Yes . . . Brooke, is it?"

Whoops. I'd been so excited for the space, I hadn't actually come up with anything. "Uh . . . we . . ."

I looked to Vanessa and Heather, who smiled encouragingly. I racked my brain frantically. What could we all talk about? Our interests were so different that we were always giving each other . . .

"Advice!" I blurted. "The Three Musketeers could do an advice column!"

Mrs. Higginbotham wrinkled her forehead. "The who?"

Several people giggled again.

I blushed and gestured at Vanessa and Heather. "I mean the three of us. I could give advice on fitness and sports"—the more I thought about it, the faster I spoke—"Vanessa could do beauty and fashion, and Heather's great with friendships and relationships."

"An advice column." Mrs. Higginbotham chewed the end of her marker.

Mary Patrick twisted in her seat to look from us to Mrs. Higginbotham. "That's not really hard-hitting news," she said. "Couldn't they do an exposé column, digging up dirt inside the school? Because I'm pretty sure there's actual dirt in the cafeteria mud pie."

"I think Brooke's idea is brilliant," said Gil, leaning over to high-five us. "The perfect balance to horoscopes. Advice from the stars . . . and advice from the students."

Mrs. Higginbotham smiled. "Advice column it is." She turned toward the whiteboard. "Brooke and . . . ?"

I repeated the other names while she jotted them in squeaky marker. The moment her back was turned, Tim Antonides sneaked into the classroom, gym bag over one shoulder.

"You must be Tim," said Mrs. Higginbotham, still scribbling away. "And you must be late."

He froze midcreep. "Sorry. I got lost."

"That's fine," she said, turning around. "Because you're just in time for your new assignment. You'll be working as an advice columnist with Brooke, Vanessa, and Heather."

"What?" Tim and I both said at the same time.

So much for the Three Musketeers.